Miss Fitzgerald

Angela Byrne

Miss Fitzgerald

Angela Byrne

NEW ISLAND

MISS FITZGERALD
First published 2014
by New Island
2 Brookside
Dundrum Road
Dublin 14

www.newisland.ie

PRINT ISBN: 978-1-84840-367-6
EPUB ISBN: 978-1-84840-368-0
MOBI ISBN: 978-1-84840-369-7

British Library Cataloguing Data. A CIP catalogue record for this book is available from the British Library

Typeset by JVR Creative India
Cover design by Mariel Deegan & New Island
Printed by ScandBook AB, Sweden

10 9 8 7 6 5 4 3 2 1

To my precious grandchildren
Lorcan, Aimee and Lauren
whom I love dearly.
And to my husband, John,
who is just the best.

Prologue

It was late in the summer of 1915 in South Africa, and the heat and humidity were at last beginning to ease. Trudy Fitzgerald was sitting in her favourite chair, in the beautiful hotel that she owned, overlooking Port Elizabeth. It was her usual evening ritual to sit for a while after her day of work. On this particular evening, she had her maid light a fire in the grate, not so much for its heat as for the attendant feelings of a comfortable home and a life well lived.

On a small Victorian table beside her was her guestbook list. Leafing through it and scanning through the names would lend her a feeling of accomplishment. As she began to do so now, she was struck by the sight of her own name: Fitzgerald. Not many Fitzgeralds had ever stayed at the Royal. The first name that accompanied it was Richard. Trudy felt her blood begin to tingle in her veins with curiosity.

'Richard Fitzgerald,' she said out loud.

She saw that the man was from Boston, USA, and travelling alone. Somewhat agitated, Trudy called Geraldine, her receptionist, to her side.

'Do you remember this man?' She pointed to the name in the guestbook distractedly. 'What does he look like?'

Geraldine struggled to remember.

'Well? How old does he look? When did you check him in?'

Geraldine looked carefully at the name.

'Miss, I cannot remember him. There are so many men here on their own. Sometimes, if they make an impression on me, I remember something, but generally not.'

'Well, we will have to find out, won't we, Geraldine?'

'If I see him, I will call you, Miss.'

Miss Gertrude Winifred Fitzgerald, or Trudy, as she was known to her family and very close friends, was a spinster who ran a busy and prestigious hotel in a magnificent building that dominated Durban in Natal. Her hotel had been built during the gold rush in South Africa, and it was truly marvellous. No expense had been spared; every detail in the hotel had been carefully thought out. There were marble floors and lavish furnishings throughout, the bravura elegance of the building matched only by the opulence of its ambition.

Miss Fitzgerald was a courageous woman who had emigrated to South Africa alone in the late 1870s when she was no more than twenty years old. At such a young age, and with no experience of travel, Miss Fitzgerald, as she was always called, had that combination of foresight and resolve that drew admiration from all who encountered her. She took her life in her hands on the day when she left Ireland alone. In those days, Irish women simply did not travel on their own, seldom even to the neighbouring county, and those who did were seen as fair game by any passing scoundrel who might want to take advantage of them. Many wondered how young Gertrude had managed to survive that first journey without suffering any serious difficulties, and, more remarkably still, without being divested of the considerable sum of money with which she was travelling. Miss Fitzgerald, though, had determined from an early age to do things on her own terms, and to approach life no differently than if she had been born a man. Even in her twenties, she was prepared to take her chances like a man and to operate without shame in what was unmistakably a man's world.

Her fellow travellers must have looked strangely, enviously and perhaps disapprovingly at the formidable young woman with the determined expression heading off to a new world. She spoke little to them, being far too busy with her own thoughts and plans to worry about what they thought of her—in any case, what other people thought of her was not something about which she generally worried.

At a time when women were supposed to just do what they were told, marrying the men their fathers chose for them, and not always with their interests at heart at that, Miss Fitzgerald was an adventurer and a crusader. Despite her years, she had been planning her trip carefully for a long time. Her father had made sure that she had been well educated, and she had indeed learned as much as possible before she left, certain that her knowledge would always stand her in good stead regardless of what she did. She had never regretted saying goodbye to Bruff, whose relentlessly dusty streets had been far too small for a woman of her ambition, and she resented the limitations that had so easily been placed on girls such as her for far too long.

The hotel was getting quiet. Few people were up and walking around. At about ten o'clock, she thought about heading to her own room for the night. As she stood up and straightened herself, she picked up the visitor check-in book and read through the names once again.

Out in the hall, a young man approached her.

'Would you mind if I kept you company for a while?' he asked her. 'It's early yet, and I don't know anyone here.

I saw you sitting alone and thought you would like some company.' Trudy looked at him, surprised.

They sat down. 'So, what business brings you here to Durban?' Trudy asked him.

As the night drew on, her personable companion told Trudy that he was an explorer and investor. He was interested in the gold mines. It was known all over the world that there were vast quantities of gold and diamonds in the Kimberley De Beers mines.

'I am here to find some of it, and hopefully make a fortune,' he said, smiling.

The discovery of diamonds in the region had brought a huge convergence of men and workers to the town. The expectation or hope of finding a fortune was widespread. It had spread like a disease, out of control. This did no harm to Trudy Fitzgerald, who could hardly keep up with the increasing demand. After all, young men with small fortunes were apt to be separated from them, and where could it be more pleasant to part company from a large sum of money than in what she had ensured were the comfortable surroundings provided by The Royal Hotel?

'Well, I can't say you're the first.' She smiled. 'We have had many men like you coming here. Be very careful who you work with. Not everybody here is honest. I've seen everything, over the years. Everything. Just be careful. Things can turn bad, or even dangerous. It can happen quickly, too.'

'Thank you for your advice, Ma'am. I will be careful.'

As they passed the time chatting about life and business while seated at the fireside, Trudy confirmed that she was indeed speaking with the Richard Fitzgerald from her guestbook.

'You seem to be a woman who has lived here in South Africa for quiet a while,' he said. 'I only arrived today. I'm trying to get to know the people and the whereabouts of the mines.'

'Oh yes, I've been here for a long time. It took me a long time. People from all over the world come here with some get-rich-quick plan or another. Let me tell you a secret: it never works that way. It takes time and effort. That's how it happened for me, anyway.'

'I know that it can take time. And you need some luck.'

'Oh yes, I've had my share of luck, good and bad. Nothing is simple, though. Nothing comes easily. Nothing worth having does. I see it every day. Some of the few who really do get rich quickly have a way of getting poor quickly too. I should know, I've seen it.'

'I believe you have seen most things from here.'

'I have every respect for people who come out here because they want to make something of their lives. But you've got to be careful. Sometimes they bring hard-earned money with them, and soon lose it all. This place has a way of doing that. I feel sorry for them, but life goes on. You can't help everybody.'

'I'll be careful,' Richard said. 'My Grandfather was a rich man. He came from Ireland poor, looking for work in Boston, as they all did back then. He worked on many jobs, and eventually became a manager of a large shipping company, Sea Faring. He left everything to my father, his only son. My father is helping with the investment I am hoping to make here. It will take me a bit of time to work out where to invest it. What would you recommend?'

'No, don't ask me,' Trudy said. 'I can't be sure what it's best to do for you. I wouldn't want to be responsible if you lost your inheritance.'

As they talked by the dying fire, Trudy found that she enjoyed the young man's company. He reminded her very much of her father, Dick Fitzgerald.

'Where did your grandfather come from in Ireland?' she asked, wondering if they were related in some way.

'He came from a place called Bruff, near Limerick. It's a small place. I believe not many people know about it.'

Trudy knew about it.

'Have you ever gone there yourself?' she asked.

'Not yet,' he said, 'but it's on my list to do. It's in my thoughts to take my aging father back there. My grandfather didn't talk about his childhood very much. I think he had a difficult time growing up.'

Trudy found her excitement hard to contain as their conversation became more animated. Her heart was beating faster as she heard Richard's words. She had to catch her breath. Throughout her life, she had always had an excellent sense of the character of a man or woman. She could suss people out, an invaluable quality in business. Now, she considered her questions carefully, sitting back in the chair and trying to remain composed.

'Do you have brothers and sisters?' she said.

'No, I am an only child.'

'What's your father's Christian name?'

'It's an unusual name: Declan.'

'Declan is a lovely name,' she said. 'It's popular in Ireland. There is a Saint Declan, you know. He came to Ireland before Saint Patrick. He is said to have landed in Ardmore in the County Waterford. Saint Declan spent most of his time praying, saying the rosary for sick people and asking God to cure them. Sometimes He did, too.'

'I didn't know that.'

'His favourite spot to sit and pray was at the back of the church beside this huge, stone bell. Folklore has it that he was leaving Ireland to return to Italy when, while at sea, he spotted this same stone bell floating on a piece of driftwood in the water. He recognised it as the same bell he had sat beside while he was saying his prayers. He decided that this was a sign from God, so he returned to Ardmore and spent the rest of his life in the priesthood. That's what they say.'

'Folklore is interesting, isn't it? You can tell a lot about people from their stories, the little bits and pieces that get passed along. I will tell my father about his saint.'

Richard Fitzgerald paused and sipped his drink. The next question he asked Trudy took her somewhat by surprise.

'So, what about your own voyage, Miss Fitzgerald? Do I detect that you are from Ireland too?'

'That's for sure,' Trudy replied.

'It's funny how people, Saint Declan and us included, love to make these long sea journeys to new worlds. I wonder why we all do it. Why did you? It must have been quite a trip.'

'It was that.'

'And what brought you here of all places? I'd love to know. If you don't mind telling me, and if it isn't too late in the day for you, of course'

Trudy bowed her head, lowered her eyes and remained silent for a few moments. Richard was concerned that he had overstayed his welcome and that he should leave.

'Wait for a few more minutes,' Trudy said. 'I don't mind at all.'

And she didn't.

Chapter 1

The woods had been in the Dillon family for generations. It was always known as their woods. In truth, it was an ancient burial ground that stood on a height and could be seen for miles. A ring of stones circled around the mound. There were many stories told about this burial ground. No one knew whether they were true, or whether it was one of those places that had a way of accumulating folklore and tales, most of which grew in the telling. Most people, however, never approached the place, feeling too afraid of the spirits and ghosts of the souls buried there. The ancient place with its stone circle and a mysterious mound covered in hawthorn bushes brought out the superstitious side of people who were not normally given to such reflections.

Many such places dotted the countryside of Ireland, and always have. Folklore and tales would be handed down from generation to generation, through word of mouth, generally maintaining that the souls of the people buried there were active in the protection of their burial place. These mounds with thorny bushes were considered by some to be the homes of the *Sídhe*, or the fairy folk. The practice since time immemorial of passing on these tales generally nourished the souls of the living more than those of the dead.

It was well known that the Dillons themselves did not enter that burial ground. Their grandfather, Michael, had gone out one morning early to work on cutting some of the trees back. The trees were so tall that they were leaning over, and were in danger of falling. Michael had heard all the stories about the mound, and was a little scared anyway, but decided to go ahead.

Michael got ready for his day's work. He had been thinking about this day's work for some time, and he said to his wife Mary that he was going to do the job that had needed to be done for a long time. Mary reminded her husband of the stories that were told, saying that she was scared for him. Michael took no notice.

Off Michael went across the fields in the pony and cart. He tied the pony and cart to the gate near the burial mound, and began rubbing the saw on a stone to sharpen it somewhat. Before he could lift the saw over his head, a branch seemed to just fly at him out of nowhere and hit him in his eye. Michael almost fell to the ground. Startled, he looked left and right and in front of him, wondering what it was. He felt the trickle of blood down his face. When he reached nervously with his hand to touch his broken face, he found his eye sliding down. It landed in his hand.

The branch had struck the side of his head with such force that his eye had come away from its socket.

Stunned, Michael picked the eye up off the ground and put it into his pocket. For a few moments he stood there, shivers running through him, in a state of shock.

Blind on his left-hand side, Michael untied his pony and cart and he made his way home. He could hardly bear the pain that ran through his eye and into his head. Looking back at the wood, he tried to understand what in the name of God had happened. He put his hand in his pocket and took out the eye, wondering at the likelihood of it going back into the socket and his sight coming back.

Then he felt a little embarrassed to enter his home, as his wife Mary had begged him not to go.

She greeted him at the door. Mary had seen him coming down the lane. She saw the bleeding from where his eye used to be, jumped into the cart and drove as fast as the pony could run them to the local doctor. Doctor John, as he was known locally, was somewhat taken aback to be handed an eye and asked, 'Can you put this eye back?'

Doctor John looked at the eye in some shock.

'Sorry, sir, that's not possible. There's no way that I can attach your eye. I'm afraid it is lost. There is nothing I can do for you, except bandage up the hole. It will close over time.'

'What will I do with my eye?' Michael asked.

'You may leave it here and I will dispose of it. Or you can take it home with you and keep in a glass jar,' replied the doctor, matter-of-factly.

'I'll leave it here with you, Doc. It would remind me of today every time I would look at it in the jar.'

Doctor John McGarry knew of the rumours about the fairy ring, as his family called it, and the danger to some people who went there. As Michael was leaving, the doctor reminded him to take great care going near the wood again.

'I will, Doctor,' replied Michael. 'You won't see me ever going near it again.'

This was Michael's second attempt to cut back some bushes, branches and trees. On the first occasion, he became violently sick. 'I vomited my guts up,' as he put it himself, the moment he entered the wood. He could only go back home, the pain in his belly growing so bad that he thought he was going to pass out. At first, he thought that it was just a coincidence, that he had eaten something that did not agree with him.

Even so, in the back of Michael's mind was the thought that it was not right to interfere with the woods. Perhaps it was some story he had heard as a young boy, listening to the adults in his home. But he was headstrong, and thought that he could get the better of whatever was going on in his wood.

Michael never went near that wood again. When he walked through his land, he would stay far away from it and bless himself three times, looking straight ahead and never turning towards it. He often felt a shiver pass through his body and a weakness in his legs, which he tried to ignore. If at all possible he would not go anywhere near Dillons' wood.

Michael also told his friends and family what had happened to him, warning them to stay away from that wood. He was nervous for his family as they were young and could stray away from him or the workmen while out in the fields. Michael put up a huge sign at the entrance of the wood, 'Trespassers beware.' He frightened his own children about it so much that they would refuse even to go into the field beside the wood.

So it was said that no one should ever enter this wild, possessed place, otherwise they would suffer the consequences, as Grandfather Dillon had done.

Chapter 2

Trudy Fitzgerald was not afraid of Dillons' Wood. She had no knowledge of anything supernatural happening there, and didn't think anything malevolent inhabited her surroundings, considering that any spirits that might exist there were more likely to be her friends. The woods were her hiding place, and she loved being there. She felt very safe indeed, and was very content to spend her time there.

Trudy felt the earth beneath her feet and the air all around her. She rubbed the sleep out of her eyes, feeling annoyed with herself. She was only eight years old. On the day before, she had left her house and crossed the wild moor from her home to Dillons' wood.

The spirits of the wood seemed to welcome Trudy. She would spend hours there, watching the wildlife. Some rabbits would come close to her. She would hold her breath for as long as she could so that she would not scare them. The birds in the air would be content to land near her, particularly the very cheeky black crows. Once or twice a little robin landed on her head and became tangled in her hair. She would put out her hand with some seeds from the ground, and some birds like the magpie would come close, then she would throw the seeds on the ground. A flock of birds would gather with a whoosh, and she would smile, happy to see them all chirping and flocking to the food. After a few months, all of the animals were no longer scared of Trudy and would come close and sniff her, while the birds would come and stand on her outstretched arms and hands.

One of the neighbouring farmers spotted Trudy heading for the wood, and shouted at her not to enter. Trudy took no notice of him, proceeding on her way, thinking that he mustn't have known these woods at all.

People who lived there would say that it was madness to enter the woods. Nobody knew what might happen. So many stories were told around fires at night. The later the night went on, the scarier the stories would get, until some people would be afraid to go home. At times, the light of a full moon would illuminate passing clouds, casting their shadows across the road.

Late on one such night, Eddie Malone—Steady Eddie, he was called—was heading home. Suddenly, he saw what looked like a dark, moving shape, stopping him dead on the road. He saw a cloud of smoke, or perhaps some sort of fetid steam, that caused him to fear for his life. Eddie was not especially given to believing in devils and demons and the like, but solitude on a dark night has a way of making believers, even of those who would dismiss such suppositions out of hand within the advantage of a brightly lit room and a little company. On this deserted road, he had neither, and was so scared that he couldn't move. His throat began to tighten, and the sweat began to prickle as it rolled down his face. His hands were shaking. He thought to scream, but nothing would come out of this mouth. He could not make out what it was he was seeing. He would later tell everyone who would listen, and many did, that it looked like the devil himself.

After a few minutes, the moon emerged from behind the clouds. Eddie could see that it was only a horse with his head hanging out over the ditch. He breathed a sigh of relief, and yet he began to run and run like the wind until he got home just the same, looking over his shoulder now and again to see if anyone was following him. 'If the moon had not shone when it did,' he would say, 'I would still be running. I was convinced that horse was the devil himself.' He even imagined horns growing out of its head, and no one would change his mind about that. The story got longer and more sinister as he told it again and again, until he was able to scare everyone. The next time he had occasion to visit the same house, he said, 'No talking about Dillons' wood tonight or I am going home early.'

Eddie Malone was not the only one who was scared to go home late at night. Often the smart lads would hide in the field and make weird noises to frighten Steady Eddie and others. Most of the time, it worked.

Dad will be so angry with me, Trudy thought. I have done this too many times, and he gets into a very angry fit. He won't get over it for days. Trudy peeped out of the side of the hole of the tree. As usual, Trudy had spent the day playing in Dillons' wood during the long summer holidays from school. She had a favourite hiding-place: a tree that had got rot and was diseased had fallen many years before, and inside it was an enormous hole going down to the roots that were now rotted through. It had been the home of many badgers and wild animals. Trudy was a solitary child, and loved to play alone.

She climbed out of her hiding-place. The herd of wild cattle, foraging for food, was gone. It was the time of the potato famine in Ireland, and humans and animals alike were starving.

Trudy made her way across the wild moor, running, occasionally tripping and falling, but she would always get up again. She did not look back in case the cattle were following her, as they had done once before.

At the house, she ran into the kitchen, where her father was sitting in his armchair.

'Jesus, Trudy, where were you all night? I went looking for you everywhere across the fields and over the moor, down by the river… not a sign of you! In the dark of night I nearly got lost myself looking for you. I shouted and shouted your name, calling you. Not a whisper I did hear, nothing. Only the call of the wild. Where on earth did you sleep?!'

Trudy did not reply. She hung her head and said nothing. Her father's eyes were swollen, and he was very tired. His trousers and jacket and shirt seemed more tattered and worn than she remembered. His shoes had seen better days. One of his big toes was hanging out over the shoe, even though he had a new pair of boots in the closet that the shoemaker had done for him last year. They had fine studs on the soles and the heels. The boots almost came halfway up his leg, and were all laced up. He was sparing them, he said, and would wear out what he had before putting on the new boots. He had a big moustache, which was going grey. His hair was receding, and growing long behind his ears. He had stubble on his cheeks. He was a tall man, slight in posture, and sat with a stoop in his shoulders.

He now sat in his usual old wooden chair, by the table that had seen better days, and which could have done with a good scrub and wash down. The floor was flagstone from the quarry. The stones were shiny and worn down in parts, especially where you entered the house and then again near the fireplace. The huge fireplace with hobs at both sides was ready to light. When you sat by the fire to warm yourself, you could see the moon and stars up the chimney, so when it rained it came down on the fire and made the embers hiss. The pork was hanging over the fire to smoke. The picture of the Sacred Heart was over the fireplace, the rosary beads hanging on the crook behind his chair. The buckets of water were on the table just inside the door. The pots and pans were under the dresser. Miller the dog was sitting at Trudy's father's feet. The stairs led up to the bedrooms, of which only two were used. To the left of the stairs, the door to the parlour was closed shut, as it usually was.

Trudy would enter the parlour now and again when Dad was not watching her. Sometimes he would simply allow her in. She loved sitting under the huge oak table with the beautiful dining chairs. There were two huge silver candelabras on each end of the table, and many silver platters on the sideboard. All the family silver was kept there. It all looked tarnished now and in need of a good polishing. In the corner by the table was a big globe of the world, surrounded by a lovely wooden frame that held it in place. Trudy was very interested in this globe. She would sit and daydream of all the countries that she would visit when she grew up. The globe would swirl around and around, and she would plant a finger on it, resolving to visit the country where it stopped. It was a game she loved. She often called her father to come and tell her about the different countries. Dick Fitzgerald loved to sit and tell her what he knew about the countries on the globe. The sideboard was full of fine china and glassware. None of this fine dining-ware was ever used, Trudy thought....

In that, she was mistaken. At one time, all of the fine china had been used. When the Fitzgerald household had an excess of food for the table, they held house dances. The ladies wore long dresses and their hair up, and they and their guests dined on the best of meats: beef, pork, chicken and pigeon, and drank the most expensive red wines. Servants waited on every guest.

The Fitzgeralds had enjoyed displaying their wealth, which within their circle of acquaintances was considerable, and cultivated friends who were similarly wealthy. Most took a keen interest in horses, and would share their stories about racing them, both wins and losses. The ladies would come down the stairs two by two, the music would start, and they would move in time with the music, stepping carefully so as not to stand on their dresses, or risk suffering the indignity of falling.

The ladies had been dressed in their immaculately laced corsets by their servants, often so tightly that they could hardly breathe, and looked very gracious. The ladies' servants who had dressed them also dressed their hair in the latest fashion, and ensured that they were impeccable before leaving the bedrooms. Each lady had a list of eligible men with whom they promised to dance, generally keeping to the schedule in so far as it was possible to do so.

Those days were well and truly over now, and the Fitzgerald house remained silent for most of the time.

It's former glory was not forgotten. Such things seldom are. Dick Fitzgerald could still recall those unbridled years, when he was a young boy, looking down though the balustrades, watching the dancers and hearing the music. Fascinated with the musicians, Dick had asked his parents to buy him a fiddle. He still had that fiddle. It was hidden in the attic now, and had not seen the light of day for years and years. At one time, when Trudy had asked her father whether he could play any musical instrument, he had replied, 'I can't remember. It's from a different time, a different world. I'm afraid I wouldn't know how to hold a musical instrument now.'

Little Trudy thought for a moment, and replied.

'It's from the same world, Dad. It's on the globe. Surely you would remember? How could you forget?'

'The same globe but a different world, Trudy, believe me. When you are young and have no cares in the world, you can remember almost everything,' Dick said, 'but when you get old, like me, and have many worries, you easily forget things.'

'Dad, don't you know I am here to look after you? I will do the worrying, and then you can remember how it was when you were young.'

Dick smiled at Trudy. How innocent, he thought. What I would give to drop all my worries and live a happy and contented life. He remembered his mother saying to his father many times over and over again: 'Never worry worries, it only worries you, it only worries others and it worries you, too.' He wishes he knew how to better follow her advice. It seemed, though, that his mother's resilience had somehow skipped a generation and emerged once again in her granddaughter.

How much easier life would be, he thought, if I could only take the worry off my shoulders and be more like them.

★★★

The scene that would return to haunt her many times in the years ahead was ingrained on Trudy's brain.

'Sorry, Daddy,' Trudy said, 'I must have fallen asleep. But I am home safe and sound. Please don't be angry with me, I didn't mean to stay out at all.'

'Well, child,' he said, 'I don't know what becomes of you. No other child that I know of goes off all day and night and does not return until morning, and you only eight years old. Don't you feel frightened or lost out at night? Wild animals could take you, and I would never see you again!'

She looked at her father, her eyes green and vivid, and her beautiful, long, curly, red hair now matted.

Trudy was not fazed by her father's words. She knew that she could go anywhere she liked, and knew that she would be safe. Next time she would stay awake, she promised herself, and would return home before sunset.

'Daddy, I am hungry,' she said. 'Is there any food in the house?'

'Over there in the bin you will find some bread, and some butter's in the tin. Help yourself. Oh, the milk is in the jug on the dresser.'

Trudy sat down to eat. The hens came in the door to pick at any crumbs that had fallen to the floor. One swish of the brush and they fluttered out, squawking. Her dog Miller sat beside her, hoping she would drop a crumb or two. He was getting old and was also hungry. Once upon a time, he had been a great cattle and sheepdog. Her father had depended on him, and he was faithful and duty-bound.

Trudy went outside, the dog following her. In the yard, there were many outhouses. Some were stables for the horses, more were for storing grain, and another for hay and yet another for farm machinery. Across the yard was a long dirt lane that zigzagged down to the road. The dog followed her. Across the lane were fields of hay and some potatoes. 'We cannot eat them,' her father would tell her.

She looked skywards. There were fluffy white clouds, and the sun was just about to come out. It was turning out to be a lovely day.

'Come on, Miller!' Trudy called. 'I need you for company today.'

I am not going across the moors, she thought. She went to the barn and sat down on the hay with Miller beside her.

She looked back at the house. She could see her father's shadow at the kitchen window, watching to see where she was off to. She knew that he was worrying about her being out all night.

James came into the barn to get the tackle for the horse. He asked whether Trudy was all right, and clearly knew that her father had been worrying when she didn't come home on the previous night. She walked out with him to the haggard field to saddle up the horse for Dick.

'Do you feel sleepy?' he asked her.

'No, not at all. Do you like Dillons' wood? I love it there with all the animals and the birds. It's so quiet there.'

James paused before answering, and looked right into Trudy's face.

'No one goes there, child,' he said. 'It is not a safe place to be.'

'I feel loved there,' she said, surprised.

'Well, you're the only one who thinks that, girl. I wouldn't go there,' he said, 'and I don't think you should either. You will torment your father. You mustn't go back there again.'

James was not married, and had no children of his own. He loved Trudy. He was the kind of person who would look out for Trudy and step in when he thought she needed help. Sometimes, during the dark evenings in wintertime, when he had finished his work for the day, he would call Trudy to his side and sit her down beside him in the barn. 'Would you like to hear a funny story?' he would say to Trudy. Excited, Trudy would grin. 'Yes, James, please tell me.'

He would recall stories from his childhood, things that happened to him in school, stories that were exchanged with his friends.

James was of slight build, tall, and always wore a heavy moustache. He wore a cap, which he lifted off his head now and then to push back his thick, black hair. His hands were huge, and hard-working. He wore heavy tweed trousers with a waistcoat, in the front pocket of which was a pocket-watch.

He wore a black, heavy coat over that in the colder months, but in the summer he wore just the one button-necked shirt.

He kept to himself most of the time. Unlike everybody else, no one in the neighbourhood seemed to know anything much about him, except for his reputation as being a good worker.

He had a tin whistle, which he kept in his breast pocket. When Trudy got bored with his stories, she would ask him to play something.

She jumped off the hay, and danced around the barn while he played some Irish jigs and reels. Trudy would laugh, while James played so fast she could barely keep up with tune.

James was the servant, and he knew his place in the Fitzgerald household. That is how he worked and looked after the horses. When he got a call from Dick, he came running. For now, anyway.

The Fitzgeralds' house was built with limestone, a huge thatched roof and a chimney at each end. There was one big door, and a side door, which Trudy used most of the time. There was also a lean-to at the side of the house, which was a dairy. Any milk and salt they had for churning butter was kept there. It was in the shade of the house, and kept cool in summertime.

Beautiful trees, mostly oak, surrounded the house. They looked hundreds of years old with their big, wide trunks, and seemed to reach to the sky. At the front of the house, over to the right, was an orchard, which most of the bigger farms in the area had. The trees all needed pruning and cutting back. So overgrown with huge briars and weeds of all descriptions had the orchard become, it was almost impossible to walk beneath the sturdy branches. It was up to James to see that at least some of the fruit was harvested from the reluctant trees.

The trees were alive with the songs of birds. During the day, the hens would often lay their eggs in the hedge at the back, so Trudy was used to going under it most evenings in fine weather to collect whatever eggs were laid. James told her that 'the cutest of hens lay out.' The rooster and master of the hens could be heard crowing loudly every morning at sunrise.

Miller stood up, barking, the hair on the back of the dog's neck standing on end. An old man entered the barn, his clothes in tatters, and the dog went for him.

'Stop, stop!' he shouted at Trudy. 'Call him back, I mean no harm, I just want a place to lie down and rest my weary bones for a while.'

'Who are you?' she called to him.

'I'm a nobody.'

'My father won't like it if you stay here.'

'Please ask him to let me rest awhile.'

As quick as she could, Trudy ran back into the house with the dog running at her heels.

'Dad!' she called. No answer. 'Oh, where is he this time?' she cried.

The workman James answered from the kitchen door,

'Your father isn't here, he has gone to the fairy man Griffin. The horse in the field is sick, and could die on us. He is gone to get the cure.'

Griffin was known to be something of a shaman.

'He won't be back for ages then,' she said.

'It'll be after dark. Is there a problem?' asked James.

'Yes, there is,' Trudy replied. 'There's a tramp in the barn and he wants to sleep and rest.'

'Don't take any notice of him at all, he won't harm us. Just leave him be and he will move on in a while.'

Such men were known as 'men of the road'. They would roam the countryside and entertain the people with stories and tricks. They were welcome enough in most households, depending upon the circumstances.

'Maybe I should bring him some tea and bread?'

'Do that,' James replied, 'I'm sure he's hungry and thirsty.'

Trudy made a mug of tea, and put lots of sugar in the mug, buttered the bread and went back to the barn to find the tramp fast asleep. Trudy left the tea and bread at his side, thinking that when he woke up he would be surprised to find the tea and bread. When she went to check later, there was no sign of the tramp, but the tea and bread were untouched. The hay where he had lain looked undisturbed.

When Dick Fitzgerald entered the Griffins' house, the fairy man was sitting at the fire mumbling to himself in a strange language.

'What do you want, Fitzgerald?'

'I am hoping you will help. My best horse is sick, and he will die soon if I don't get medicine for him.'

Griffin stood and went to a small door beside the fireplace, speaking in a language that Dick Fitzgerald did not understand. Dick was stuck to the floor. After a while, Griffin started pulling something like a rope from the small door beside the fireplace. Though Dick did not understand, he knew that the shaman, in his trance, was somehow using the rope to help the cure to work, all the while talking in a different language. He then asked Dick to hold the rope while he mixed a concoction in a jam jar.

'I want you to mount your good horse and return home. Do not speak to any person, and don't dismount, otherwise the spell will not work, just get home as quick as you can.'

A little unnerved, Dick Fitzgerald began the journey home with the medicine in his pocket, his horse's hooves crunching into the ground beneath with each step. He met many people on the road home, and in turn unnerved them through his silence. The moon was full, brightening the night sky, glancing off the white frosting on the grass.

When he got back, James put the horse into the stable. The sick horse was lying down, quiet and still. Dick was concerned that it was too late for any medicine. Nevertheless, he administered the medicine as he had been told. Exhausted, he went to bed for the night, very tired after the long day.

The first thing he did the next morning was to go out to the sick horse.

To his surprise, the horse was standing and pawing the ground with his hooves, eager to get out into the field. He was back to full health. The cures that some of these men had were simply unbelievable, he thought. They were somehow from a different world, an older world, whose secrets were now known only by very few. The same globe perhaps, but a different world just the same. So long as you believed in the Shaman, the spell would work for you.

Dick woke Trudy up and told her about the horse. She was pleased; she knew that the horse meant everything to him. Later she told him about the tramp wanting to rest and sleep.

'Did you look after him, Trudy?'

'Yes, Father, I did.'

'Oh, that's good. If you hadn't, I don't think our horse would be alive now.' Trudy asked why, but Dick said that he would explain later, as he had to go out now and see to the cattle.

That night, before going to bed, Trudy asked her father to explain about the tramp. Dick tried to put it into words she would understand.

'Well, if people were good to the likes of a tramp, it would help them with other things in life, like us with the sick horse. If you hadn't taken care of him, he could maybe cast a spell and our horse would not be better now.'

'That's all very strange, Daddy. How can that happen?'

'That's the way of the world, Trudy child. Always try and do good for everyone,' Dick answered. 'Say your prayers every night before going to bed, and again when you wake up in the morning. Prayers will help keep us all safe.'

Trudy persisted.

'I always say my prayers, but it didn't stop something really big happening to my mother. That's not fair.'

'Your mother had nothing to do with this, Trudy. She had an accident.'

'Yes, I know,' Trudy replied impatiently, 'but couldn't God still have kept her alive for us?'

'Maybe God wanted her and it was her time to go,' said Dick.

'I wish she could have stayed here with us, Daddy.'

'Oh I know, child, but that was not to happen.'

Trudy looked down at her shoes.

'I don't like what happened to Mammy. She should be here with us. I miss her so very much.'

Chapter 3

Before the Famine, people kept pigs for their own use, which were slaughtered every couple of months. The meat was salted and kept in a barrel, while some was put over the huge fireplace to smoke. It was a big occasion in the household, everybody helping out; everybody with a job to do.

Bob's Mary, as she was affectionately known, was passing into town on her donkey and cart. It was a weekly trip for her. She did the weekly shop, which consisted of grain for the hens, and flour and wholemeal to bake bread, sacks of each being thrown into the cart. The flour came in white cotton sacks, which the women of the house would boil in washing soda over the open fire in a big pot to remove the brand name on the sides of the bags, then carefully sew them together by hand to make sheets and pillowcases for the beds.

During the week, Bob's Mary would spend her time looking after and cooking for her two brothers John and Mick.

Bob's Mary was promiscuous. She really didn't know any better. Their parents were long gone. It was only Mary, John and Mick. None of them ever married, which caused some talk and speculation in the neighbourhood.

Bob's Mary liked to smoke a dudeen, or small clay pipe, which she had in her mouth most of the time. Her mouth was stained from tobacco, and when she smiled all you could see were brown teeth. When she went to town, though, she wore fiery red lipstick and the reddest rouge on her cheeks. Trudy discovered that Bob's Mary was using the cooking bags of flour as face powder.

Bob's Mary had many men friends who called to her from the road, as she and her brothers lived a fair distance away from the road down a long lane. The usual call was a whistle. Then she would be seen crossing the field and onto the bank of a hill, where she would meet with whomever was calling at that time.

Most people thought that there was a little lacking in her; that she was not the full shilling. Others thought that she was not a full woman or man; that she was born in between, or that she was not capable of having children at all. There was always talk about Bob's Mary. She was the most noted person in the district, hated by the women and found very interesting by the men, many of whom despised her every bit as much, even whilst enjoying the pleasures of her company.

Trudy was fascinated with her. Bob's Mary in turn was kind to Trudy. On the evenings when Trudy came to visit, she would stay until nightfall and Bob's Mary would walk her home. They had great fun together. Trudy would gather the eggs and help with making the tea. The kettle was hung over the fire, where it would take ages to boil. Bob's Mary would sometimes bake bread and churn the butter. They would sit together and eat.

On one evening, when Trudy was coming home from school, she crossed the fields and went to visit Bob's Mary. In the kitchen, Trudy noticed the bag of flour and the twig, which Bob's Mary rubbed at the back of the fire and then put the black stuff on her eyebrows. The lipstick and blusher came from red crêpe paper she had, which she wet with her spit and then applied to her lips and cheeks.

'You can't stay, Trudy,' she said. 'I won't be here long, I am going to visit a neighbour. So you have to go home this evening.'

Bob's Mary went to the end of the lane with Trudy, then she stopped to have a wee. Trudy could not believe how she did this. She just stood with her legs apart, and the water gushed out like it would from a horse, Trudy thought, leaving froth on the ground.

Dick Fitzgerald told Trudy not to go to Bob's Mary's house any more.

'It's not fit for young girls like you. She is not the right person to visit.'

Trudy wondered what could possibly be wrong with Bob's Mary. With no one to ask, though, Trudy just did what she was told. But she missed the company and fun she had on the way home from school, and would look down the lane and hope that Bob's Mary would be coming up towards the road. Trudy tried in vain to whistle like the men she heard. She would purse her lips and blow as hard as she could, but nothing happened. Then she got a blade of grass and, like she saw James doing, put the grass between both thumbs, and blew. A loud screeching noise came out, something like a wild hare in the night, or like a fox defending its young.

Trudy tried blowing so hard that she cut both lips with the sharp blade of grass. When she saw the blood, she stopped, wiped the blood away on her sleeve and went on home defeated.

★★★

Dick Fitzgerald had been a widower before. He had married young, to a lovely girl named Catherine Hogan. They both lived in the same townland of Bruff, in County Limerick, and were neighbouring farmers. A match was made by the parish priest, Father Henry, as he always did for big farmers. Dick was happy to be fixed up with a recommendation from Father Henry, as he knew that his father before him had depended on the parish priest to pick a bride for him.

The bride was also quite happy to be chosen by the priest. Love did not come into it at all. Nevertheless, after some years they cared deeply about each other and shared companionship, home and children.

Dick and Catherine started a family straight away. They first a son called after Dick's father Martin. The next year they had twin boys, Declan and Noel. The boys were much loved by their mother. She would stand up to Dick if he was getting angry with them; she could see no wrong in them.

After school every day, Catherine would sit down together with her sons and ask them how their day had been. She was interested in their schooling as she could not read and write herself. She often asked Martin, the eldest, to read his schoolbooks for her, especially his history and English books.

The younger boys would also listen to the stories. Whenever Dick came in unexpectedly, he would put a stop to the reading and tell the boys to get out in the yard and start feeding the cattle and bringing in the sheep. He had no time for learning out of books.

'You learn the hard way,' he said to them, 'books will get you nowhere.'

Martin would protest that it was a great achievement to be able to read and write. He asked his father what he would do if he had to sign something.

'Sure you wouldn't have a clue as to what you were signing. You could be giving the farm away and you wouldn't know it.'

'What do you think the law is for, Son? That's why we pay them to look after our affairs. My father before me did not know how to read and write, and he got along fine in this world. He was a very good farmer and a clever man.'

'That may be so,' Martin countered, 'but the world is changing and being able to read and write is the best thing ever.'

Martin eventually convinced his father, and got Dick to learn how to read and write. Catherine and the younger boys looked on, and they too learned the skill, albeit indirectly.

All was well for the Fitzgeralds for fifteen years or so, until Catherine fell ill.

She was sewing bed sheets together one day, when she got up suddenly to answer a knock on the door. Her scissors fell to the floor. She tripped and fell on the scissors, which cut deeply into her upper arm.

She put on some iodine and bandaged the cut. That night it got very sore. She washed in salt and water and put more iodine on to soothe it. Each day it got worse, until one day Dick sent for the doctor, who came to the house on the following morning, only to find Catherine burning up with fever. She had blood poisoning.

The doctor gave her some medicine, telling her to take it three times a day. When downstairs, he took Dick aside.

'Dick,' he said, 'it doesn't look good for Catherine. I don't think she will last until morning.'

All that night, Dick sat in the bedroom with Catherine and said many decades of the rosary. Not once did she open her eyes. Dick wanted to tell her that he would look after the boys and see that they did well, that he would find good matches for them, that they would marry and live on the farm with him, or that perhaps he would be able to buy them another farm.

He wanted to assure Catherine that everything would be taken care of. He also wanted to tell her that he would continue farming and would always remember her. Catherine never opened her eyes. Eventually, he whispered in her ear everything he wanted to share. He could hear her breathing becoming more laboured, and a rattle in her throat.

Early the next morning, Catherine sat up in the bed, opened her eyes wide and looked around the room. Dick was delighted.

'Oh, Catherine,' he said quietly, 'were you having a sleep?' But she seemed not to hear him, or notice anything.

She lay back down on the pillow with a long sigh. Dick hoped that she would take in another breath, but as the moments went by, it was obvious that Catherine was gone. Her head slipped sideways on the pillow, and Dick saw that she had a slight smile on her face.

For a long time, Dick would remember how she held her face and her head every time he came into that room. He never slept in there again. He moved to the room across the landing, within earshot of the boys, who slept in the room next to Catherine's.

The wake began on the next day. Mrs Winston came to lay out Catherine in a shroud of white satin and lace, and did her hair up in a bun as she had always worn it.

As in life, Catherine looked beautiful. Dick put her rosary beads between her crossed fingers and laid a single red rose at her feet. He had bought her the best teak coffin that money could buy.

It was a devastating blow for Dick and the boys. They missed their mother terribly. But at least they were now grown enough to help their father on the farm—their farm.

Chapter 4

The sons were also very much afraid of the room in which their mother had passed away. They eventually developed a habit of running past it, blessing themselves with the sign of the cross and whispering a prayer to God to keep their Mammy safe and in his kingdom, until they would eventually meet her once again in heaven.

Dick had no choice. Time passed. The children grew, and two younger boys, the twins, decided that they would emigrate to America. Most of their friends had gone already, as there was very little work to be got. They wanted adventure, and hoped to make a better life for themselves in the United States of America.

On the farm, there was not enough work for all of them. The boys were tired of the same routine every day with very little money to spend. They couldn't wait for the day to come. Almost every night they discussed their plans. Where they would make their home in the states, which state had the most work available. They wrote to their friends to find out what work was like and how were the wages.

A lot of their friends who had made it in Boston advised the twins of work that was to be had, and what kind of life they might expect. 'Come on over,' their friend Stephen Wall had replied to the latest letter, 'Don't waste any more time, we are all waiting for you here.'

They went into Limerick City to the shipping company, made plans and booked their one-way tickets. Queenstown to Liverpool, then wait in Liverpool for two days for the ship sailing to New York, then catch the train to Boston, where Stephen Wall, Pat Cody and Jim Walsh would be there to meet them.

Three months later they had the American wake in the house. All the neighbours came to visit and see the boys off. So many people were leaving Ireland for America and other parts of the world, often to say goodbye forever. Many would stand on the deck of the ship and look back at Ireland as they sailed out to sea, knowing that they would never return to their homeland. They could only look forward and hope that what was to come would be a lot better. Even so, they knew in their hearts that they would miss their family, friends and home.

The boys took a handful of soil from the field, put it deep down in the pockets of their long coats, and left Ireland, never to return. All that Dick could hope for was that they would get there safely and alive. Please God they would have a better life in America.

★★★

Eddie Malone, Steady Eddie, who thought he had seen the devil by the side of the road but realised it was in fact a horse at a gate, came originally from Clonakilty, County Cork. He worked for the Dillons as a farm labourer and servant. He was reasonably happy there. The days were long and the work was hard, but he was well able for it, he said. There was no work in Clonakilty at that time, and his mother had too many mouths to feed.

He was the eldest of eight. He heard that his family had grown bigger, and that now there were eleven in the

Malone family. He sent home whatever money he could when he got his wages at the end of the month. He knew that his mother did not have much. She was a kind-hearted woman who would refuse no one. Anyone who came to the Malone household were always asked in for a cup of tea, and got whatever else was going at that time. In Eddie's mind's eye he could see his mother struggle every day to feed her family, and going without herself, so that the children would not be hungry.

Eddie's father was a delicate man who smoked a pipe and did little else. He had about two acres of ground, where he grew vegetables, but not the potato. Not then. Eddie's father would sometimes hunt for rabbits, or fish in the river. His mother was a good cook, and could make a dinner out of nothing, or so Eddie maintained.

Eddie owed most of what he earned to the local shop, where he spent it on tobacco and porter. He had an eye on Margaret, one of the Dillon girls. She looked so handsome with her jet-black hair, which swung down her back almost to her rear end. Her eyes were luscious dark brown, and she also had a lovely figure. He loved the way she walked and held her head to the side. Her smile could light up what was otherwise, to Eddie Malone, a rather dreary world.

Margaret Dillon rode out on one of the horses every morning. Eddie was always there waiting for her. He would saddle whatever horse she was going to take for a ride on that day, making sure that he had everything right for Miss Dillon. He would watch for any chance of a smile from Margaret. Mostly she did, but it was out of habit more than anything. Eddie meant nothing to her; he was a servant and a farm labour. There was no way that any of the Dillon girls would entertain a farm-hand or servant. They were just waiting for a big farmer to come along and wed them, but before getting their father's advice and approval.

Eddie did not stand a chance, and in his heart he knew that. A man can dream, he would say to himself. I will find a beautiful wife, he would tell the boys he met up with at night. He seemed in a hurry to find a woman to marry. He wanted to settle down and have a family himself, he told the lads. If that did not happen, then he had it in his mind to set out for America, Canada or Australia. A wife could be found there, if not in Ireland.

Indeed, everybody seemed to be leaving. And little wonder. The redcoats, as the British soldiers were called, would commonly trawl the farms under instructions from the lords and the barons with one thing in mind: to take the land and force the farmer to give up his home. A small sum of money was paid out to evict the farmer, confiscating all the animals, especially the horses. Other farmers would be given a one-way ticket to America, Australia or Canada, where they would have to go, whether they liked it or not. Many farms had already been confiscated, families could not pay the rent they were asked to, or provide the landlords with goods or animals they demanded. Many of the landlords were ruthless, although there were said to be some who looked kindly on the people and gave them a chance to pay or come up with the goods they wanted.

Some families just abandoned their homes, walking away when things became impossible to manage. Those families carried nothing with them but their children, and took to the roads. They begged and lived rough. They were the most pitiful sight. So thin, with unwashed and tangled hair. Those families, who had a relatively good life before the landlords, were now destitute, ending up on the roads with nothing.

Families could be seen around a camp fire beside the road, trying to keep warm with some sticks from the ditches. Some even ended their miserable lives on those roadsides. These sights frightened other, luckier farmers, who feared that they might meet a similar fate.

Fear can be a powerful motivator. All did their best to keep on top of the farming, tried to keep their thin animals fed, and worked in the fields every day until they could work no longer.

The British had not yet arrived at the farm of Dick Fitzgerald. He knew from his friends and neighbours of the ruthless treatment of which they could be capable, and was afraid for his future. Minor crimes were treated as major ones. There were even stories of farmers working in the fields being shot for no more cause than the look on their faces or the way they talked to the British soldiers.

Dick was cutting hay in his own fields one afternoon when he heard a commotion in the far distance. He ran to the highest point and looked over the countryside. To his horror, he saw his neighbour Tim Dowling and his son Eamon being dragged across the field. The soldiers were shouting and raising their rifles. Dick could hear their words carry on the wind. 'If you don't tell us where you live, we will shoot to kill.' A shiver of fright came over him as he realised that they would do the same to him. He decided, there and then, to get out as quickly as he was able.

He ran back home like the hounds of hell were at his heels. There is only one thing for it, he said to himself. If these hooligans of soldiers come anywhere near here, I will take them down. It will be self-defence.

High up in the chimney, Dick had two rifles hidden, bound in white cotton sheets that his mother had made specially. He now loaded them and prepared to fire. He had more ammunition hidden in a box under the bed, also covered with an old coat that belonged to his father.

Dick then called in his workman James. James entered the house wearing a forlorn expression. Dick sat at one end of the table and James at the other.

'Have you heard anything about the British soldiers coming and confiscating the land belonging to the farmers?' Dick asked.

James had heard a rumour concerning a farmer miles away. He outlined what he had heard locally. Stammering slightly, he said, 'They are ruthless, they are taking everything they can get their hands on, including stock and any grain farmers might have.'

'I've seen it too', Dick said.

'Ah they will never come this far,' James continued, 'it's only the farmers near the town whose land they want. Nothing will happen out here, they won't walk this far in those heavy uniforms.'

'That's what you think, James,' said Dick. 'I was out on the field overlooking the Dowling family farm before you came. I heard shouting and a row going on. When I went up the hill to have a look, I couldn't believe what I saw and heard.

'Mrs Dowling was pleading with the soldiers to leave and stop taking their food or her family will starve, that the redcoats were trespassing. The soldiers pushed her and one of them brought down the gun on her head. The husband tried to protect her by lying across her body. They hit him, too, until the blood was running down both their faces. The soldiers warned them that they would be back, that they would take their land, one way or another. They had no mercy for anyone. Then they looked around in all directions. I was scared for my life, and all I could think was to run back home as fast as I could. I got the rifles down from the chimney. We are ready now if they come here. I'll stay here and I'll never give up. Why should I leave my home and farm that's has been with the Fitzgerald family for hundreds of years? My father handed it down to me, and it's mine to hand down to my children when the time comes. It's not for the British or their lords and masters.'

Dick was white in the face; James could sense his terror and anger.

'Sir, I will stand beside you, we will fight together,' said James. 'We will have to work out a plan of action.'

And so they set about working out what they would do if anyone came to the house or the field. Dick decided that if he were out in the fields, like he had been on that day, then his signal would be the whistle he carried in his pocket at all times, and James would do the same if the soldiers came while he was working in the fields. The whistle would be blown hard three times. The other would then be alert as to what was going on.

They would also bring a tin mug and a spoon, and bang the spoon off the mug and make a racket. They would be heard on a still and quiet day, but if the wind were blowing in the wrong direction, then they could not be sure whether they would be heard or what would happen.

Whenever action was needed, though, the one nearer to home would run and get the guns, and get to whoever was in the field as fast as they could. Dick did not know whether James was a good shot, and it had been some years since he himself had practised. They were taking a considerable risk.

They did not want to practise. If shots were heard it would cause concern for the neighbours, and might alert British soldiers. The British lords had 'befriended' one farmer, giving him large sums of money in gold and silver in return for informing on their neighbours. Where there was one, there were sure to be others. The talk among the community was that the Rafters were spies.

It was a game of wait and see.

Dick was afraid for the safety of his home and farm, and started carrying the gun at all times. James tried to tell him not to as it was drawing attention, but James' advice fell on deaf ears. In the end, Dick had James follow him everywhere he went, also with a loaded gun, but James would have to walk alongside the road in the ditch, where no one could see him, while Dick walked on the road. The ditch could be very rough, and the going slow. Dick would stop and stand in silence every now and then, listening for any unusual sounds or sights, sometimes calling to James, 'Hold up here.'

On occasions when a voice could be heard in the distance, Dick would become agitated, saying to James 'Is that them? Are they coming?'

'No, Sir,' was his usual reply. 'It's only the Sullivans bringing in the cows.' Or 'It's only the wind you are hearing.'

'Are you sure, James?' Dick replied. 'Are you sure? I heard them.'

James spent a lot of time reassuring Dick that there were no redcoats around.

When they finally got back home, Dick was exhausted, both from carrying the rifle and from the stress of listening for sounds and different voices. He would throw down the gun and flop into the chair beside the fire.

James would fill the kettle and hang it over the fire to make the tea.

'It's a terrible thing, living like this, James. It's a terrible thing to live in fear.'

For years, Dick did not know how his sons fared on the coffin ships, until one day he received a letter from Declan.

The letter was like gold, a rope thrown to a drowning man. With shaking hands, he opened it. They had made it to Boston, had found work on the docks, had a nice room in a boarding-house and were enjoying life in America. Even though the work was hard, and the hours long, it was still better than Ireland. They mentioned that they had met up with Eddie Malone—did he remember Steady Eddie at all? Dick smiled. Of course he remembered Eddie.

In the letter was a bank draft for one hundred Irish pounds. Dick felt tears of both happiness and sadness welling up in his eyes. That letter was read over and over, again and again. Dick was considering joining the boys in the States, leaving the farm to his eldest son Martin.

Then Dick's life took a different twist.

Dick's oldest son Martin found a nice girl in Tipperary, a farmer's daughter and only child. It was a match made in heaven, and she was the love of Martin's life. They married, and lived on the Tipperary farm. Dick did not stop his son. He wanted him to be happy, and gave the marriage his blessing. Nevertheless, it was unusual for the eldest son to leave the farm that he would eventually inherit. The proposal of marriage from the Tipperary family seemed too good to pass up. Martin had made his mind up to go. He did wonder about his father, and how he would manage without his help, but he knew that he had a faithful servant in James. Also, in the back of his mind, he thought that Dick would leave him the family farm too, and in the end he would be the owner of a farm in Limerick and another in Tipperary.

Dick took out his best suit, tie and waistcoat, and got his hair cut by the local man who cut hair for most of the men in the district.

Martin had the tailor make him a fine three-piece suit. He went into Limerick to get the cobbler to make him black leather boots. Father and son were dressed well for the big day.

It was a small wedding. Mass was at eight in the morning with a few neighbours and friends, with a simple gold band for his new wife to show the world that they were married.

When Martin saw his new bride entering the chapel, his heart skipped a beat. She was a natural beauty. She wore a long green wool tweed dress with a lovely gold broach in the collar in the shape of a rose. She wore a matching green hat that tilted to the side of her head, with net that covered her eyes, and dark green leather gloves on her hands. She was a picture to behold.

She slipped her arm into Martin's, and walked to the altar where Father Sean was waiting for them.

When the marriage vows were taken, his new wife lifted the net that covered her eyes. She smiled. Martin could hardly contain his excitement.

After the marriage, they went on home, changed their clothes and worked for the rest of the day.

Chapter 5

Dick was now alone. The parish priest called to visit him one morning, and suggested that he marry again, recommending a young farmer's daughter half his age.

'Oh, Father,' he replied, 'I don't know if I would be able to keep up with a young woman at this stage in my life. I've already buried Catherine.'

Father Henry convinced him that Margaret would bring new life both to him and the farm.

'She is full of energy,' he informed Dick.

'Give me time to think about this, Father,' Dick replied.

Dick was not a man given to rushing into anything, and so it was only after long contemplation that he realised that he was indeed lonely, and missed the company of a woman, and of his family too. He did not want to disappoint the parish priest, and felt beholden to him somehow. All he had was the farm servant James. There was no conversation to be had out of James, but he was respectful to his master and did not gossip. He did his work, and the only time he would ever enter the house, other than to take his meals, was when an animal was sick, or when a cow calved.

A month later, Father Henry was back. He chatted for a while about nothing in particular. After several minutes,

Father Henry stood up straight and fixed his coat. Then the question came. Dick knew that it was coming.

'Well, Dick,' he said, 'have you considered my proposition?'

'I have, Father... I have thought about nothing else. It's gone through my mind day and night.'

Dick had dwelled on his thoughts and memories of Catherine and the boys, going through everything they had done together. Catherine had known him inside out. She had worked hard to make ends meet, worked on the farm and kept the house. She was there for them all when they needed her. Those memories will never be erased from my mind, he thought. He sat down on his wooden chair. Father Henry sat at the table.

'Would you like a cup of tea, Father?' Dick enquired.

'Ah, no thanks, Dick, but if you have a drop of the creature, I will have some.'

With that, Dick pulled out a bottle of poteen from the press with two dusty glasses.

'Fill them up!' said the priest.

The two men drank the spirits down in one go.

'Ah,' said Father Henry, 'that's good stuff. You must have a good supplier.'

'I drink very little these days,' replied Dick. 'Only for medicinal purposes. That bottle was there a long time to mature.'

'Well now,' said Father Henry, 'we will get down to business. Have you decided yet?'

Dick took his time to reply. After a long pause, and a sigh, he did.

'I have indeed. I would like to meet Margaret, if you would kindly set it up. I don't want to buy a pig in a poke.'

'Do you think I would do that to you, Dick? You know me better than that.'

'All the same, I would like to meet her first.'

The conversation grew more serious. Dick told Father Henry things, sometimes only learning of his own feelings when he heard them expressed back to him in Father Henry's words.

'It feels dishonest. It feels as if I didn't love Catherine enough.'

'But you did, Dick. Everybody knows that. She would not have wanted you to suffer for the rest of your life. I can see that you have suffered.'

'Maybe Margaret won't want to marry me when she sees me. I am much older.'

'I know. You said that before. Meet up with her. What do you risk?'

A month later, Dick went to meet Margaret Dillon at her parents' house. He put on his best Sunday clothes, washed and shaved and groomed his moustache. He called James to ready the horse, telling him that he would be gone for the day.

James was concerned about his master. It was unlike him to head off for the day. Dick had not told him where he was going. James thought that Dick was going to look at a horse or to buy some stock. They were short of hens, too. Or he might come home with some geese to fatten up for Christmas.

Little did he know that Dick was going to meet a new woman. Dick kept his plans close to his chest. He knew that he would be the talk of the town, so no one would know until he made his final decision. He did not want to encourage the chatterers and gossip-mongers, and knew all too well that, in those groups, a little encouragement was all that was needed.

At the Dillons', Dick tied the horse to the fence at the side of the house, giving it the bag of hay he had brought with him. He had a good look around and took in everything in the yard. Not bad, he thought. Not bad at all.

With a confident stride, he walked towards the door of the house, which was painted in an emerald green colour. He straightened his coat and stood as tall as he could.

He knocked, then waited for the door to open, which seemed to take forever. He did his best to pull himself together, painfully conscious of his years. He knew that he did not have to go through this if he did not want to; it all depended on whether he liked the girl. The door opened. Margaret, or so he assumed, stood in front of him. She was beautiful, and, for a moment, words failed him.

'Come in, Sir, we are waiting for you. Isn't it a grand day?' she said.

They sat together in the parlour for a while. The parlour was bright, with a green settee and two armchairs, an oval table with carving on the legs in the middle of the room, and a dresser with beautiful china and some crystal glasses neatly stacked up by the wall.

There was one huge window, from which you could see the mountains in the distance. Dick remarked that the view was breathtaking. The fireplace was glowing, and you could feel its heat from across the room. It was very cosy.

Margaret seemed shy, like all young girls do, and after a few minutes the parents entered and sat on both armchairs. They introduced themselves, and were very pleasant indeed. Every now and again, Dick could feel their eyes burning into him, sizing him up. They wanted to be certain that he was an honourable man, even though they were very happy with Father Henry's suggestion. They knew that he was much older than their daughter, but that did not matter too much—he had, after all, a good farm with a lot of acreage. They would miss Margaret, but did not want her to remain a spinster. It had been difficult to find a husband for her.

The Dillons knew that it was essential to find a husband for Margaret. Father Henry had pointed out to them how lucky they were to get such a good match for their daughter. He also reminded them of what might happen to Margaret if she were to remain unmarried. Girls who failed to find husbands had a way of disappearing into institutions of one sort or another. Families with all daughters and no sons were particularly at risk. There were hospitals to take care of such girls, and many of them never emerged again from such places.

While the Fitzgeralds lived in fear for the safety of their farm, the Dillons feared for the safety of their daughter. If she remained unmarried, it would be a convent for her at best, joining a religious order, or a hospital if she were less fortunate. They had heard about the hospitals for girls, and heard rumours of how many of the girls in their care never left those God-forsaken places. They were spoken of in the same hushed tones that were once reserved for the woods.

Margaret would, they feared, struggle in a convent. Some convent orders were very strict and had a vow of silence, which could prove challenging for a young girl. Some could remain silent, but some just could not stand it and would eventually leave. With a little money from the Reverend Mother, they would emigrate to foreign shores, unbeknownst to their family. It could be many years later before the family would get a letter from their daughter, letting them know that they had left the convent and emigrated.

Fear can be an unforgiving master, and the Dillons feared the shame that their unmarried daughter might bring upon them, whether by abandoning a convent, or abandoning the world entirely. No, Margaret was to be married, and Dick Fitzgerald had just walked through their door.

Why risk the embarrassment of her going into a convent and then leaving it, as she was all too likely to do. They would never be able to forget about it. They would be talked about.

On the other hand, at least a daughter in a convent was likely to be safe. What harm could come to a girl in a convent? That, though, would mean not seeing her for perhaps seven years, until the day of the final vows. The Dillons had seen it happen: painful partings of parents and daughters bound for the convent. A family in the next townland had five daughters, none of whom could find a husband. The parish priest's services had even been called on, but despite his best efforts, he could not come up with anyone. All five were fine girls and worked hard for their parents, but there were just too many girls on the one small farm.

A father of daughters could seldom enjoy untroubled sleep. Of the few options that presented themselves to the Dillons, Dick Fitzgerald was clearly the best, advancing years or not.

The conversation was limited, and there was little being said beyond Dick's questions and Margaret's nervous replies. She seemed pleasant enough, was of a sturdy build and was tall. Her black hair and dark brown eyes gave her a striking appearance. Dick stayed for about an hour, making small talk.

Margaret, meanwhile, was hoping that Dick would say yes, even though he looked as old as her father. She was anxious to have her own home and a family, and she knew that Dick Fitzgerald was an honourable man, and would do the right thing by her. She was interested in

Dick's home and house, she couldn't wait to see it. She envisaged herself as the woman of the house, with all the cooking and washing to be done, and most especially as Dick Fitzgerald's wife, for having the name was a great thing, or so Margaret thought. Father Henry, she decided, knew exactly what he was doing. Choosing her meant that she was better than the rest of the young women in the townland.

Margaret knew that her parents were delighted and happy for her. She was, after all, marrying well, and into a good farm with a history of wealth in the family. For the next month or so she would have to wait for word as to whether the marriage would go ahead or not. She dreamed of what she would wear on the day and how the ceremony would be. She promised herself that she would be a fine wife, but would never mention Dick's first wife Catherine. She would show the greatest respect for her. Margaret didn't want to know anything about Catherine at all; she was going to put her stamp on the home and make it the way she wanted to have it. The prospect of a new house was at least as exciting to Margaret Dillon as the prospect of a new husband.

For days after the meeting, Dick could think of little else but Margaret Dillon. He did not want to tarnish Catherine's memory, and was troubled by it, despite Father Henry's reassurances. He wondered what the boys would think of their father marrying again. Then again, the boys had their own lives now, he thought. They are grown, and one married, and the twins in Boston. He decided against consulting with them.

Finally, after characteristically detailed and lengthy consideration, Dick made the decision to marry. On the next month he went to the Dillon household and asked for Margaret's hand. Father Henry had been to the Dillon household many times, and on each occasion had heartily recommended Dick Fitzgerald. The priest had told her parents that she could do no better, that he was a good man and that he would make a good husband. He had a good farm and was proud of it.

The Dillon parents had questions for Dick. Would he look after Margaret? Would he not work her too hard? Given his age, if he were to go before her, would he leave the farm to her? Dick answered all their questions, and agreed with their requests. Nonetheless, he was uneasy about leaving the farm to Margaret, and refused to commit to this. Despite this, his reassurances proved sufficient, and her parents' consent had been obtained.

'We will marry in the spring,' he told the Dillons. 'That's three months away. It will give us time make all the arrangements.'

So the date was set for the wedding. With both apprehension and excitement at the thought of having a companion and the company of a woman in the house, and also someone to cook and clean for him, Dick went to town to get a new suit from the tailor. He already had the new boots, of course. The parents of his bride-to-be made arrangements with Father Henry.

The morning of the wedding came around quickly. It was a lovely spring morning, the sun was up and everywhere Dick looked seemed brighter with every moment.

He arrived at the chapel half an hour early to be there before Margaret. Father Henry came out of the presbytery to wish him good health, good fortune and a happy marriage before the Mass began. Dick and James were dressed in suits.

James had scarcely spoken a word all day. He was in a mild state of shock, but could not show it to his master. James had not expected Dick to get married once again. Ageing and set in his ways, it seemed an unlikely move to make at his stage of life. Dick had only informed James about Margaret, and the wedding, a few days before, and James had been struggling to adapt to the idea of there being a new woman in the house. Everything was sure to change. James did not particularly know Margaret Dillon, and he and Dick had an established routine around the home.

There was little that James could do about any of this. He could only watch his master and friend marry this new woman whom he knew only slightly better than James did. James could only hope for the best.

He was, after all, the best man.

The altar was lit up with candles burning. Prayers were offered to favourite statues, coins were deposited into the collection box, and candles were lit, often accompanied by thoughts of someone special, or a special intention or hope.

The two men sat in silence, just staring at the altar. They stood up when they heard hushed voices.

Margaret came into the chapel, her parents and sisters behind her. She was dressed in a purple coat and hat. Dick looked at her with smiling eyes. She walked up the aisle confidently, her father close by her side. Dick stepped out into the aisle and took Margaret by the arm. They both walked to the altar, where Father Henry was ready to begin. Dick was very nervous, his hands were shaking and he could feel a trickle of sweat roll down his face. He tried to hide it by rubbing his sleeve across his forehead.

Margaret stood as still as a judge. She listened intently to the priest's words. She took the vows very seriously.

The marriage took place just before the Mass, and then everyone waited for the Mass to end. They lingered outside the church until the entire congregation had left.

The family stood around making small talk to Dick and James. Finally, Dick said 'It's time to make a move, it's getting cold standing here.'

He looked at James, and pointed to the pony and trap. 'We will be off now,' he said to the Dillons. With that, the couple got into the trap, and James sat at the front and drove the pony.

Dick had given his house and yard a quick, half-hearted clean on the week before the wedding, to have it looking a bit respectable for the new woman. He cleaned out the ashes from the fireplace and gave the floor a good sweep, having watered it down first. Outside the front door were sticks and timber blocks that James had cut and prepared for the fire. He moved them to the shed, pulled some weeds and briars from the side wall of the house and brushed down cobwebs that hung from the roof to the ground. That was about the extent of what he could do.

The newly married Mr and Mrs Fitzgerald returned to Dick's house. Dick took Margaret on a tour, a little embarrassed at the state of everything. He tried to explain that he did not have anybody to do anything for him, and that he was not much of a housekeeper.

She was not impressed.

'Well, we are just going to have to start somewhere. And why not today?'

In her trunk, amongst all her belongings, she had a lovely patched bed quilt that she had made with her own hands. She also had two fine lace tablecloths and some embroidered pillowcases, all her own work.

'The first thing I have to do is start cleaning,' she told Dick. 'I cannot cook a meal in this house until it is cleaned up.'

That night, Dick told Margaret that the big room was hers and that he would sleep in the middle room. Margaret was taken aback at this, and wondered why he did not wish to sleep with her. Perhaps, she thought, he did not like her.

So Margaret spent the next few days cleaning and polishing, cooking for Dick and James.

Chapter 6

Father Samuel Henry was originally from County Galway. He was the eldest son of Brigid and Thomas Henry, and came from a farming background. His parents had over one hundred acres of good land bordering Mayo. They were a big family, with ten children in all.

Samuel was always a devout Catholic. His parents wanted him to be a priest from a young age, and he was given great encouragement, while growing up, to become a priest. Most big farmers had a priest and a nun in the family. It was as near as you got to a passport to heaven. A priest for a son and a nun for a daughter would be a particularly devout gift to God. It was a statement of their thankfulness for all their worldly goods, and also an expression of hope for the future that their son or daughter would pray to God to keep them safe and not fall on hard times.

Imagining that he was doing so of his own free will, at the point when he finished school at the tender age of seventeen, Samuel duly joined the priesthood and began in the seminary. Both parents went with him to settle him into the college.

When it was time for him to leave the seminary and enter the priesthood, his mother was delighted. The bishop ordained sixty priests that morning. When he took his final vows, all the family were there. He seemed disconnected from his siblings, and they in turn felt distant from him.

Like most mothers, Samuel's own mother adored the son who would be the priest.

Samuel had been a clever boy growing up. He had helped his parents on the farm. As an adult, he was everything a priest could be. He was designated for the African missions, where he would spend ten years. Saying goodbye to his parents and family and heading to Africa was a daunting task; he embraced it regardless, and was happy to serve God.

On Father Henry's return home, ten years later, the hard work in Africa had left him a different man. He looked different—he was heavily tanned and he looked well. Bishop Thompson decided to send him to the parish of Bruff in County Limerick, where Father Henry remained and became a pillar of society. He took his faith seriously, and expected his entire congregation to do the same.

Father Henry was known for his intolerance of any unfaithful person in the parish, sometimes going so far as to actually get on horseback and follow any couple who were not supposed to be together. No couple was 'supposed to be together', as he saw things, unless he had personally arranged the match. This he intended to do until everybody in the parish had been suitably paired up.

He often berated a man and woman for being out courting at night, and would send them home to their families. At Mass, he would then be red-faced and in a temper, pounding the altar to drive home with his ceremony the Word of God.

Most parishioners were afraid of him. If the priest called to their door, they were petrified that their children had done something wrong. On the other hand, all the parishioners called on him to make a match for their children, and were usually happy with the choice the priest would make.

Father Henry considered that once he had matched a couple together, that they would then be indebted to him thereafter. He would sometimes continue to call on the people he had matched together, even many years after the event. Father Henry was lord and master of his congregation, and was used to being asked for advice on almost everything.

He was asked to pray for good harvests, pray for rain, pray that farms would thrive and sons prosper. His involvement in every aspect of the lives of the people in his parish made him like a father to them all. The wealthy farmers in the parish would support the priest by giving him money, also donating towards the upkeep of the chapel. Usually you would see a pew at the top of the chapel with an inscription: Donated by the Murphy family, or whoever it happened to be. When these particular families attended Mass, they had their own seats. No one would dare to sit in their pew.

There were some customs among the Irish people that Father Henry would not allow, such as the belief in fairies, leprechauns, and banshees, which was common. Pilgrimages to holy wells were frequent. Fairies were generally considered malevolent, although they sometimes performed beneficial functions. The leprechauns were considered to be small, mischievous male spirits. A pooka was actually a fairy who generally took the form of a dark horse with yellow eyes and a long, wild mane. The banshees, *bean sídhe*, woman of the fairies, warned of approaching death with unearthly wailing.

Dick Fitzgerald's first wife, Catherine, thought that she had once heard a banshee. On one night in particular,

Catherine had been visiting a neighbour's house. There was a new baby in the home, and she had knitted a cardigan for it to bring as a gift. She had talked her way through the hours, and night was falling as it was time for her to leave.

As she made her way home, a storm was coming. She heard the loudest clap of thunder, and lightning lit up the road in front of her. She started to run fast, and just as she was coming towards the lane up to her home she heard this awful wailing call. She was sure it was a banshee. It put goosebumps on her arms and sent a shiver down her spine. She was stuck to the spot and could hardly breathe.

She knew what it was. Someone in the area was dying. This awful, shrill call was unnerving Catherine, who thought that she would never get home quickly enough. The banshee was following her as she ran up the lane to be home. Inside the ditch on her left-hand side, the shrill, wailing bawl came again, so loud this time Catherine put her two hands over her ears.

Another big streak of lightning lit the lane all around her, and then the loudest clap of thunder.

Catherine ran as fast as she could into her home, the sweat dropping off her face. She went straight to her husband for reassurance that it was not any relative of theirs.

'Oh, Dick,' she said, 'the life was frightened out of me with that banshee. I never want to hear her again.'

Dick sat her down and comforted her, reassuring her that the banshee would do her no harm at all. It was just what they do when someone is going to the next world, or so they say.

Catherine stayed in the house for the rest of the night, terrified. Dick reminded her of the old man at the Neary farm, who was not well. Perhaps his time had come.

Dick said he would go to the Neary household on the following morning and pay his respects. When, early the next morning, Dick made his way on horseback to the Neary family, it was as he thought: the old man had passed away on the evening before.

The family asked him in, and down to the parlour where the corpse was lain, all fitted out in a white shroud, rosary beads intertwining his fingers. He looked at peace. A feather was used to spray holy water over the corpse.

Every hanging clock in the home was turned towards the wall, and mirrors were covered with a black cloth.

Dick was made a fuss of by the Nearys, of course. They offered him tea and stronger refreshments, which Dick had accepted in honour of the old man. The family were seated at each side of the corpse, some in tears, others saying silent prayers.

Dick sat with the family for an hour, talking of the old man, how he was a good father and how hard he worked to keep his farm. They were all remembering together how good this man was and how fortunate they were to have him for a father and grandfather. His loss would be felt for evermore.

Banshees, according to Catherine Fitzgerald, were very real, and the death of Neary proved it. Dick's new wife, however, was not nearly so sure.

In the time between the marriages of Dick Fitzgerald, the Church had expanded, and was making its presence felt, particularly in the west of the country. Dick had seen changes during his life, changes of beliefs, and of habits of thought. This was not all a matter of calm introspection; the law had altered, and the relaxation of the Penal Laws had enabled the Church to build new churches and establish schools. As Dick was beginning to feel his age, he saw priests and nuns taking control of the education of most of the Catholic population.

The world that Dick had known and grown up in was changing, and he was not sure if it was for the better. The traditional wakes, the belief in fairies, dancing at crossroads and other such ancient practices were condemned by a newly energised and empowered priesthood, who sought to encourage new ways of life. They encouraged devotions such as the Way of the Cross, novenas, the veneration of the Sacred Heart, parish altar societies, sodalities, confraternities and temperance associations. A practice sprang up whereby the priest went to local villages to say Mass and hear confessions. It was a day-long event, with a gathering in the evening for tea, singing, story-telling, music and step-dancing. Where Catherine had believed in a loosely connected tapestry of folklore and myth, Margaret was part of a new world, her faith of a new and more regimented type.

On one warm, balmy night in August, Father Henry was out after dark on horseback with his Tilley lamp in his hand. He was on a mission to search out courting couples, taking it upon himself to keep his parishioners in line, as was his way. He worked tirelessly to keep everyone under control, and wielded considerable power and influence over the lives of the people in his congregations, with most of whose comings and goings he was well acquainted.

On this particular night, however, Father Henry wasn't having much luck in finding courting couples, until he was on his way home at around midnight. He was just back at the chapel when he heard a screeching sound coming from the graveyard. He pulled up the horse and stayed as quiet as he could. He heard it again. He dismounted, and entered the graveyard. As Father Henry stumbled over a headstone, he heard the screech again. This time he knew that it was human, and not a hare as he had first suspected.

Over in the right-hand corner, there was a sloping ditch to the next field behind the graveyard. Father

Henry quenched the lamp and continued in the darkness, stumbling over more headstones. When he got near where the sound came from, he lit the lamp once again. He held it up high and saw two people sitting on the ground.

'Get up,' Father Henry shouted, 'and step over here!'

To his astonishment, he heard a female voice.

'Put out that light, you are blinding me!'

The priest did not take too kindly to that.

'Step up, or I am coming down on you with my whip,' he responded.

Bob's Mary stepped out into the light. Looking dishevelled, pulling at her blouse, she did not take kindly to being interrupted by the priest.

'Is that you, Father Henry? God, you frightened the life out of me!'

'What are you doing out this time of night?'

'I thought you would be in your warm bed and not out here in the middle of the night. You have to be up early every morning to say Mass. You should be well asleep by now.'

Ignoring Mary's comments, Father Henry shouted, 'Who is that man with you, Mary?!'

'What man? Sure there's no man there, you must be seeing things,' she chided.

'You were hardly alone here in the graveyard, Mary. I know you have someone with you.'

A moment or two went by, and who should stand up to the light but the townland's biggest farmer, Joe McGee. Mary told him to go back where he was, and that she would handle the situation. Joe McGee just stood, eyes cast down, his hair all over the place, buttoning his shirt. With his hands shaking, he was not doing a good job of it at all.

'Not on your life,' said Father Henry. 'I want to talk to the two of you. Come on now, both of you.'

He ordered them out of the graveyard, saying that it was a mark of respect for the dead.

'It's a mortal sin to behave like this in this graveyard! Of all the places around here, why did you choose where the dead are laid to rest?'

'Ah, Father,' Mary said, 'we were safe here. We thought no one would find us. Sure, the souls here would not harm us.'

Both Bob's Mary and Joe McGee were like two scolded children. He ordered them over to stand by the chapel door.

'Now, Joe McGee,' he said, 'you have brought disgrace on your wife and family. Say the ten commandments for me now, go ahead.'

As Joe McGee reached 'Thou shalt not commit adultery,' he balked and turned his eyes up to heaven.

'God forgive me,' he sobbed, the tears rolling down his face.

When it came to the ninth commandment, Joe was slow to say 'Thou shalt not covet thy neighbour's wife,' finding the words hard to speak. He turned to Father Henry.

'She is not anyone's wife. She lured me here tonight.'

Bob's Mary gave Joe a dig with her elbow into the stomach, which knocked the air out of him. Father Henry wouldn't believe any of that.

'I am sure she did not twist your arm. And as for you, Mary, will you ever stop taking on other women's husbands?'

Bob's Mary turned on the priest.

'Would you get away out of that! I do nothing to any man; they come looking for me. Don't you know that I am the finest woman around here, Father? Joe here is looking for me all the time. He says I am great and a lovely woman.'

Joe just looked at the ground. Father Henry was furious with the two of them.

'What have you to say for yourself?' the priest said.

'Sorry, Father. I will not do it again.'

The priest puffed out his chest.

'I'm afraid you have done enough for me to feel compelled to let your wife and family know.' 'Oh please, Father, Joe McGee pleaded. 'I will make it up to you. I will buy another pew and put into the chapel.'

'Not enough for me to forget this night,' Father Henry replied.

'All right then,' said the dispirited man. 'I will give a donation of one hundred pounds next spring.'

Mary stepped in.

'No you will not, Joe McGee. You will give it to me for all the good times you had with me. You never gave me money,' said Mary, 'and there you are offering one hundred pounds to the priest! Come on now, hand it over to me,' Mary said.

She shoved him in the back, and he nearly fell to the ground.

Father Henry did not know what to do with Mary. He warned her not to come out at night like this.

'I will not be so lenient on you the next time I find you out courting married men, or any men for that matter.'

He told the two of them go home and go to their beds.

'I will do what I like, Father. You can't stop me!'

With that, Mary decided that she was not tired at all, and she didn't want to go home yet. She didn't feel the cold, and was used to it. Joe, on the other hand, couldn't wait to leave and run home. Despite the size of him, Joe McGee was terrified of that priest. He made a run, jumped out over the wall of the graveyard and disappeared into the night. Bob's Mary was left standing with the priest.

'You come with me, Mary,' he said.

He tried to lecture her on what she was not to do, and make her promise that she would stay at home at night.

'But that does not include the day,' she said to the priest.

'Sure, what would you get up to in broad daylight?' asked the priest in some surprise.

'Ah, sure, you would be surprised, Father,' she leered at him.

Mary bade goodnight to the priest, and promised to return home.

When she left the chapel yard, she went running on the road thinking she would catch up with Joe. With some distance from the chapel, she shouted for Joe McGee.

'Wait for me!' she shouted, panting at the same time.

Joe was gone, and there was no catching up Mary could do. She walked on home in the still of the night, and could hear the cry of an owl and the swirl of a bat or two around her head. Mary was not afraid of eerie sounds or sights. She would chat to herself and often sing to herself. She had ways of entertaining herself without the company of a man, although she found their company preferable.

On the next Sunday after Mass, the priest had a letter for Joe. Joe was to sign the bottom of the letter, promising that he would pay the church the money the following spring. Bob's Mary had cost him dear. Bob's Mary was there too, staring up at the priest while he was giving the sermon

She was unsure of the priest, and wondered whether he might say something about finding a couple in the graveyard. He had made such comments before, leaving the congregation wondering about who it might have been.

Father Henry had found many couples in awkward and compromising situations out at night. The priest was determined to seek out courting couples and make matches for the big farmers. He wanted to be in control of all matrimonial decisions. His zealous fervour was tireless, and everyone would go out of their way to avoid him, especially after dark. As he continued to ride out at night on these self-imposed 'missions', courting couples seemed to become fewer and fewer, which to him was a sure sign of God's approval of a job well done.

Chapter 7

'Dick Fitzgerald,' Margaret called to her husband after a week sleeping alone. 'What kind of a marriage is this? I did not marry you to sleep alone in my bed. I might as well not have married you at all.'

Dick reddened.

'Margaret,' he said, 'I thought I was a bit old for you. I am well past having more children. I married you because you are a fine girl, and to keep me company.'

'I am not for just looking at,' she said. 'I wish to have the company of my husband in bed at night.'

It was with a sense of nervousness that night that Dick entered Margaret's bedroom.

He seemed uncomfortable getting into bed, wearing his long johns. That went on for a few nights until he turned to his new wife and said, 'Will we have a go?' And so the marriage was consummated. Dick got the hang of doing the act once again and with someone new, and looked forward to being intimate with Margaret every night from then on. Margaret had great energy, and Dick kept up the pace with her. He began to get more energy for the farm work. Margaret was bringing out the good in him.

It never occurred to Dick that Margaret would fall pregnant. He got the shock of his life when, after three months of married life, his wife announced that there was a baby on the way.

'Oh my God,' said Dick. 'How did that happen?'

'You know well how it happens,' said Margaret.

Margaret was quietly over the moon about the baby. It would make them a family, and she was hoping to have even more children with Dick, though she was not about to tell him that now.

'But I am too old to have children! What will everyone think of me? I have my family reared and my eldest son is married himself. We will be the talk of the neighbourhood. I will be the oldest father ever known in this county!'

'Well,' said Margaret, 'you are not too old in bed with me. You will have to deal with it, there is nothing we can do now. I am happy and you should be happy for me.'

'Well, I have to get the cot down from the attic, if it wasn't thrown away years ago. You will have to make the baby clothes yourself.'

'That's no problem for me,' she said. 'Now I want to let my parents know.'

'Wait,' Dick said, '... wait a while until I get used to the idea myself, don't be too hasty. Sure, there is no hurry in letting them know.'

'I am bursting to let them know. It's just great, it's all I ever wanted, a child of my own to love and care for.'

'Next month,' said Dick, 'we will call and stay for the day, and you can tell them in private.'

Margaret worked hard, and did not complain at all. She blossomed with her pregnancy, and was looking forward to the arrival of the new baby. She began to knit little coats by the open fire at night. She also knitted blankets and made cot sheets. Dick would sit opposite Margaret just watching her.

'Do you want a boy or a girl?' he asked her one night.

'Ah, I don't mind, Dick, whatever God will bless us with. How about you?'

'Well, I have the three boys, so I don't mind if we have a little girl.'

Time went by quickly. As Dick had promised, they went to visit her parents and tell them of the baby. The Dillons said that they had been hoping that they would hear news like this soon. Margaret's mother offered to come and stay when the time got near. Dick was not too sure. He was not used to having one woman in the house, let alone two; but he had to agree for Margaret's sake.

When Bob's Mary got wind of the news that Dick Fitzgerald was going to be a daddy again, she called in one day on her way home from town. She met James in the yard. With a wry smile on her face, she asked James whether it was true that there was a baby on the way in the house.

'I know nothing,' James said.

'Ah, you eejit, everyone knows. She's in the family way. Dick Fitzgerald must have something between his legs after all. It is not a sausage, sure?'

'Don't be talking like that now, Mary.'

'Imagine him fathering a child again after all these years. Sure his sons are all grown and gone to work!'

'Why are you so interested in Dick Fitzgerald and his wife?' James said.

'Ah, I thought he was well past having children, that's all. Won't it be a big upheaval in the house with a new child?'

James walked away with a gimp on him. Mary shouted, 'Wouldn't you like to be a Daddy yourself, Mr James? I know what all you men like.' James looked back over his shoulder and told Bob's Mary to go home and look after herself.

'Maybe I will come back later and keep you company. Wouldn't you love to have me by your side in the frosty nights to keep you warm?'

'Be off with you now, Mary,' he said.

Bob's Mary turned and walked out of the Fitzgerald yard, chuckling to herself about Dick and the new baby. She brushed back her hair and headed for home.

Bob's Mary took a keen interest in the arrival of any new babies into the district. The fascination was chiefly regarding how, and by whom, they had been made. It brought a smile to her red lips and a devilish grin to her face. Some say that she'd had one herself and didn't know what to do with it. She was said to have wrapped the baby up in some old clothes and left it at the gate of the church in Limerick city. The story was that the baby was found by the nuns and taken in. It was supposed to have been a fine healthy baby girl. Such stories never went away, Stories like this were told and retold, and the sins of the past were never allowed to be forgotten.

As the baby grew strong inside Margaret, it kept her awake at night. When she lay down, it would start to kick and often kept going for an hour or two. Getting closer to her confinement, Margaret was uncomfortable and her back began to hurt, and she would sit down more to rest, yet still she managed to keep up with the housework, baking and cooking.

One Saturday evening, she was washing the dishes after the dinner when she felt her waters breaking.

'Dick!' she shouted. 'Come here quick; go get my mother and the nurse! My time is here.'

Dick called to James.

'Get the horse ready, fast as you can, it's Margaret. Stay with her until I come back.'

When Dick got to the Dillons', they were about to go to bed. Mrs Dillon went straight for the bag she was bringing and got her coat and hat from the crook at the back of the door.

'Hurry,' she said to Dick, who was talking to his father-in-law. Mrs Dillon and Dick rode on horseback.

'How far is she gone?' the mother asked, concerned.

'Not too long,' Dick replied with a sigh. 'I have to call to the nurse on the way back.'

'I hope we are not too late. It's her first; it could come quickly or may take a long time, no one knows.'

They got the nurse out of bed, and when she saw who was there, she knew that it was time to go to the Fitzgeralds' house. As Dick and his mother-in-law waited for her, every moment seemed like forever. When the three of them eventually got to the house, Margaret was lying on the bed and James was in the kitchen boiling a kettle of water over the fire.

The nurse first asked Margaret about when the pains started and how long ago. Margaret saw her mother coming into the room.

'Mammy!' she called out.

'You will be fine,' her mother said. 'I have given birth to ten of you, it will be no bother at all.'

The birth was slow, and continued all night and into the next day. Eventually, a lovely baby girl with red hair came into the world.

'Beautiful, she is!' cried Margaret's mother.

The nurse picked her up.

'She is a fine healthy baby, Mrs Fitzgerald. Put her to your breast now and get her used to sucking.'

'Mammy, call Dick, let him into the room with us,' said Margaret.

Outside in the hall, Dick was sitting on a small stool with his head in his hands. He raised an eyebrow and asked if it was a boy or a girl.

With tears in her eyes, Margaret's mother replied: 'It's a lovely girl, Dick. Now you will have two females in the house.'

'I will have three for a while. Oh, she is so small,' he said, looking at the baby.'

'No, she is not,' said the nurse. 'She is a fine strong eight pounds, a good-sized baby.'

That night, all four in the Fitzgerald household slept soundly. With Margaret's mother to help, Dick continued as normal. Mrs Dillon did everything for Margaret and the baby, for which Margaret was grateful.

'Mammy, what would I do without you to help me? I want you to stay on with me for a month or two.'

'I can't do that, Margaret.'

Mrs Dillon reminded her daughter that she had to go home and look after her father and the rest of the family.

'You know I feel welcome here, and would love to stay with you, but I will have to go home soon. You will come and visit us often, and we will look forward to seeing you and Dick and the baby.'

'Don't go yet, Mammy, we have to christen the little mite yet.'

Margaret wondered if her younger brother Stephen would be the godfather, and if the Fitzgeralds' neighbour Mrs Meany's eldest daughter Anna would like to be the godmother.

'Well, Margaret,' Mrs Dillon said, 'I know that Stephen will, but you will have to ask Anna Meany yourself.'

Later that day, Margaret tucked the baby under her shawl, and went down to the Meanys. It was her first time to visit the house, but she had met Mrs Meany going to Mass on a few occasions, and Mrs Meany had invited Margaret and Dick to visit.

Of course, Dick was always too busy to go anywhere, and Margaret did not like to go alone. She strolled into the Meanys' yard, to be unexpectedly confronted by three vicious-looking dogs. On hearing them bark, Mrs Meany came to the front of the open door with her new baby in her arms, and what seemed to be a crowd of children behind her.

'Down, down dogs!' she shouted, and with that they retreated back into the house.

'Come in,' Mrs Meany said. 'You are welcome. Where is Dick, did he not come with you?'

'No,' Margaret said, 'he is busy ploughing the uplands, and won't be back till dark.'

'Have a cup of tea with us. That is all we have to offer you; we have no food in the house.'

'I know,' replied Margaret. 'The tea will be fine.'

The women sat at the table with an audience of children looking into their mouths.

'Go outside and play,' Mrs Meany told them. 'Children should be seen and not heard.'

They went outside, and continued to peep in through the crack in the door.

'Mrs Meany, I'd like to ask your daughter Anna whether she would stand for my baby. The christening is next Sunday. I have to make arrangements with Father Henry.'

Mrs Meany fussed over the baby, and was visibly moved by the suggestion that Anna should be her godmother. Eventually, she couldn't help but cry happy tears.

'Oh, Margaret, she is beautiful, with that lovely red hair, and those lovely eyes. She is a big baby too.'

Mrs Meany put down her own baby girl in the little bed in the bottom drawer of the sideboard beside her, and took Margaret's baby in her arms.

'Maybe these two children will go to school together? Wouldn't that be grand for them?'

Margaret wasn't thinking about school at all. She wanted to get the christening over first.

'Anna will be this lovely baby's godmother, and she will be very good to her,' Mrs Meany assured Margaret. 'What will be her name?'

'Gertrude Winifred. But we already call her Trudy.'

Chapter 8

As time went on, things became worse in the Fitzgerald household. Dick did his best to provide food and a warm fire for his family. He killed a pig every couple of months, and Margaret made the best of every bit of meat from the pig.

Dick never again slept in Margaret's bed, no matter how much Margaret pleaded with him. She was lonely. Dick was good to her, but when it came to companionship at night, that was gone for good.

Margaret, being young, was in need of love and affection. At night, when Dick had gone to bed, she turned to James. She would slip out to the horse's stable and call him. At first, James was shocked.

'Is something wrong with Dick?' he asked her.

'Ah, not at all, James,' she replied. 'He is well asleep by now.'

'So what do you want?'

'Nothing at all,' she replied. 'I just wanted a little company and conversation.'

'Don't come to me for that, go down to Mrs Meany,' he told her.

'How can I do that in the dark of night?' she replied.

'Well, I am no one to be talking to. Go back into your house and leave me be, the boss will sack me if he finds you out here with me,' he said, unconvincingly.

'Ah sure, he won't know I was here at all,' she replied.

'Go on now,' he said, 'back to your bed.'

As Margaret walked back to the house, James stood looking at the fine woman Dick Fitzgerald had, and yet preferred to sleep alone. He would love to talk with Margaret, although he had not spoken to any woman in years. He kept his head down and did his work. It was the only way to maintain his sanity.

The next day, Dick called James in for dinner. Gingerly, he came to the table, cap in hand, almost afraid that Dick knew about the night before. James sat in his usual spot at the end of the table next to the door. Margaret was at the fire, taking off a big pot of gruel. Dick asked James for an account of the animals and the state of the stables.

When James heard word stable, he looked shocked. Dick noticed his change of expression.

'What's the matter? Have you something to tell me?'

'No,' he replied.

'Jesus, I thought something was gone wrong out there. You look like a ghost.'

'No, Sir,' he replied. 'Everything is fine. Nothing new to report today.'

Looking under his eyes across the room at Margaret, he thought that she would be the death of him. As quickly as he could get the food into his mouth, he was up and off out the door.

Dick turned to Margaret.

'What is wrong with that fellow today? He's acting like a lunatic.'

'Don't mind him at all, he has days like that, as you know.'

'Well, he's been with me for years, and I have never seen him look so frightened.'

The week went by, and Margaret and James never spoke a word. Secretly, James was longing to talk to her, hold her and make her feel loved. He guessed that Dick was not bothered to love her, like he could. Yet James dared not make a move, he did not feel worthy of her.

James Donovan had come to the Fitzgerald farm as a farm labour, one of many looking for work. He convinced Dick Fitzgerald of his experience by speaking very knowledgeably about every detail of a working farm. James had said that he wanted to make a new start. He was a hard worker, and well able to take instruction. His big interest was in the horses, and he said that he had seen none finer than the animals out in the paddock on his way into the house.

Dick Fitzgerald decided to give James a chance.

'All right then,' he said, 'I will give you a month's work, without pay. If you prove to me that you are the best man for the job, then I will consider taking you on full time.'

James was delighted, and vowed that he would make Dick Fitzgerald very pleased to have given him the chance. Dick watched James closely every day. He could see no wrong in James; in fact, James was the best workman he had ever employed. Every day, James did the work of two men, if not more.

After the month had passed, Dick summoned James to the kitchen table.

'Sit down, James,' said Dick, pointing to the chair at the end of the table. 'The month is up now, and you have proved to me that you can handle the work here.

'You will sleep in the loft over the stables, where you will be nice and warm during the winter. The heat from the animals will be fine for you. I will continue giving you your daily meals. Just one thing, James: there will be no days off. We have to work here every day. Every Sunday we will be going to Mass, so you will almost have a day of rest, but you will still need to tend the horses and bring in the cows for milking. Your wages will be ten shillings every month. I want you to think about this for a while, come back to me and let me know if this is suitable for you.'

It didn't take James long to consider Dick's offer. Even so, James waited for a week to pass before letting Dick know that he would stay and work for him. He also asked for five shillings more in his wages.

At this, Dick hesitated. For a few moments, James tensed up, not knowing how Dick Fitzgerald had taken his request. The last thing he wanted was to sound ungrateful.

'Well,' Dick replied, 'you are worth it if you keep doing the work like you are.'

'That I can promise you, Mr Fitzgerald, Sir,' replied James.

Dick Fitzgerald had no knowledge of James' past or background, and James was not about to enlighten him.

When he started to work for Dick, James looked like a man who had lived well and was knowledgeable about world affairs. As time went by, though, James became withdrawn, hardly lifting his head from the work he was doing. He made little in the way of conversation with his employer. Although the Fitzgeralds made the workman welcome, he always kept his distance. James had a past, there was no doubt about it, and no one knew much about him in Bruff.

James worked long and hard. It was a way of hiding out and starting a new life for himself. James and his two brothers Michael and Joseph had been involved in a bank robbery in which two men were shot and killed. They were bank clerks, and had tried to steal from the bank.

The Irish police were looking for the three men for murder and bank robbery. Each of them had gone in a different direction to lie low until the search was over. They had got away with a substantial amount of cash, some in different currencies. The brothers pledged to meet in ten years' time in Dublin city, where they would not be known.

James had always intended to return home after a few years, and so did his brothers. But there were Wanted notices up in every bank in the country with a picture of the men. A substantial reward was offered for information about their whereabouts.

The wish to return home to meet up with his brothers had diminished with time, and James was happy to stay on at the Fitzgeralds' farm. He never knew what happened to his brothers. The money was hidden in various places so as not to risk all of it being found. He would carry some of it in his boots, wrapped in newspaper to keep it dry. That way, he reasoned, even if he should need to make a sudden run for it, he would have enough. Every now and again, he would take it out from his boots, look at it and count the money again. It brought him mixed feelings. He would never be able to forget about what he had done in the past; not so long as his guilt needled him daily underfoot.

He had worked his way through the money, bit by bit. In time, only what he carried in his boots remained. Knowing that he needed to start again, he had made his way to safety in Bruff. In the winter, the boots got so wet that the newspapers and cash became damp and began to smell. He asked the first Mrs Fitzgerald for old newspapers. When she wanted to know what they were for, he replied that he wanted to put lining in his boots.

'I have some cardboard,' she had said. 'It's a box I don't want any more. You can use it for your boots. It will be much better than the newspaper.'

That night, James sat in the loft and cut out two pieces of cardboard to fit inside his boots perfectly.

He pulled out a stone from the wall behind his head where he slept. He then carefully put the old newspaper full of cash into the hole, and replaced the stone. He felt that it was a very safe place for his money. He would occasionally take the stone out and check it.

It used to bother him at times that he had not seen his mother and father again, knowing that they may have gone to their final reward without a word from him. James had got into a rut, though, rationalising his actions as such men will, and in the end had little desire to make contact with his family. Only trouble for him lay in that direction, or so he told himself. When push came to shove, James had decided long ago that he could only truly rely upon himself in this lifetime.

He often went over the day when they robbed the bank, and would relive every moment of the raid, thinking of ways in which they could have done it differently. They might have got more cash from the bank, and kidnapped the staff, instead of killing them.

His younger brother Joseph had been nervous, and had taken the first shot, killing the clerk. All hell broke loose from there. James jumped over the counter and got into the back office, where the door to the vault was wide open. All he had to do was fill the bag that he had under his coat as quickly as he could.

If he were to do it again, he would plan the whole thing himself. James was the oldest brother; he should have taken full control of the raid. Instead, he had let his brothers convince him that their way was the best. James felt little remorse. He felt that robbing the bank was his life's achievement, and would do it again if he had to. He worked harder than most, and often for much less in the way of reward. He deserved his share of what life had to offer. That is how he justified his actions to himself.

That was back then. He was a different man now, living like a hermit, dour and withdrawn. His appearance was unkempt and ragged, his pocket-watch pawned. He looked like a man suffering from deep depression. Little remained of the man who had once arrived at the Fitzgerald farm in search of work.

Chapter 9

Dick Fitzgerald's prize mare was in foal. The mare and her foal were very important to Dick and his family. His horses were a way of making money for him. Who, after all, was not in need of a good horse?

After about ten and a half months, Dick started to keep a close eye on his mare, putting her in the stable at night. James was told to listen out for any movement, and Dick would get up many times to check on her. He let her out in the field during the day, where the whole family kept an eye on her.

It was very tiring for Dick. Margaret came to the rescue.

'Dick,' she said after dinner, 'you go to your bed and I will keep vigil tonight. I have a gut feeling she might give birth tonight with the full moon. If anything happens, I will call you, and sure James will be on hand too.'

At around eleven, Margaret went out to check. She had decided that she would stay up all night. When she entered the stables, James was alert.

'Why are you coming out here at night?' he asked her.

'I'm on duty tonight,' she replied.

'But sure it is no place for a woman to be.'

'Well,' Margaret replied, 'Dick is exhausted and is in need of a good night's sleep. I'll call him if anything happens.'

James looked seriously at Margaret.

'Are you sure you are all right here? I can keep watch like I always do.'

'I promised Dick,' she said, 'so I will stay.'

Margaret checked the mare.

'I will stay with you for company,' James said. 'Sit over here on the bed of straw, there is a cold draught coming in the door where you are.'

Margaret sat down beside James. She could feel the heat from his body, and could smell his sweat. His hands were rough, with dirt ingrained into them. She could see his face with the light of the full moon beaming in through the cracks in the roof.

'How do you live out here all the time?'

'Ah, sure, I'm used to it. I prefer to be here. It's my own little place. I can lie here and think about the day's work and what is to be done tomorrow.'

She sat quietly, listening for sounds, but all she could hear was James' breathing gradually getting faster.

Just then, Margaret felt movement beside her. It was a huge rat.

'Oh Jesus!' she shouted, and moved closer to James.

James instinctively put his arm around her.

'I hate those things,' she said. 'Are there many out here in the barn?'

'Not too many. When the cat comes they scuttle away.'

James kept his arm around Margaret, and she did not protest. After a while, he put his hand on her hair and stroked it softly. Margaret turned her face towards him, feeling his breath on her face. They kissed. It was not long before they were making wild, passionate love, all thoughts of wrongdoing completely forgotten. For those few moments, locked together, their selves and their concerns dissolved into the eternity of lovemaking, and they found some refuge in each other's bodies from the vicious and cold outside world. While they were together, nothing else mattered.

What they did not know was that Dick had got out of bed to check on Margaret and the mare. He saw them. He stayed very quiet, and afterwards heard James sobbing.

'My God, if my master knew this, I would be gone from here forever.'

Margaret felt more confident that it was never to happen again. They had not, she thought, been seen or heard by anyone. She reassured James that everything would be fine, that Trudy was asleep, and Dick too. If it were ever known, she would be humiliated, as would the whole Fitzgerald family. Her own people would disown her. Yet the danger in doing something risky thrilled her inside. She reasoned with herself that Dick would never ever know what was happening.

Dick slipped back into the house, and into his bed. He did not like confrontation. But he was shocked. At that moment, he did not know what to do. He lay there wondering. What would the neighbouring farmers think of his marriage? How foolish he had been to take this young woman for his wife. Father Henry made me do this, he said to himself. But for him, I would not have married again. Now what will I do?

And now the child. He had not been lying there for long when Margaret came to the door, shouting.

'Dick, Dick, come quickly, we have a fine colt foal! Come see for yourself!'

Dick got up out of the bed and dressed again as though he had not seen anything untoward.

Dick wasn't the only one who had seen Margaret and James. Never one to stay at home dozing by the fireplace,

Bob's Mary was also out on the prowl that night. She had been out walking and heard laughing and commotion in the Fitzgeralds' barn. When she slipped into the yard, and quietly stood listening to the goings-on in the barn, she felt jealous, wanting to be part of the action. She knew, of course, that they were playing with fire, judging by the way the two of them were carrying on. Mary chuckled to herself as she moved on into the night. Margaret, you scamp, she thought. If Dick only knew what you and James were up to.

Bob's Mary had just left and was out of sight when Eddie came walking past too, on his way home from the rambling house. In the quietness of the late night, he too heard the cries of passion. He looked into the barn, and saw James and Margaret in the act of lovemaking. Eddie was stunned at what he was seeing and hearing and stood amazed. He couldn't drag himself away from the barn. They were finished by the time he had regained control of himself. Out he ran like the hounds of hell in case he was being watched. When he got far enough away, he slowed down, breathless. What would old Dick think about that, he thought.

Dick was glad to see that both of mare and foal were fine and healthy. The foal was up on all fours now and in search of its mother's nipple. Dick stayed in the stable, both arms on the railing, just looking.

The next morning, Trudy came running and tumbling into the barn.

'Mammy said we have a new foal,' she cried out. 'Pick me up, Daddy, I want to see.'

He picked her up, and she stared in awe. She wanted to go in and pet the new foal, but her father said no. The mare would not be her usual self, and might jump on the child.

'I only want to rub the baby foal.'

'Not just now, Trudy,' said Dick. 'The mare is protective and you might get hurt.'

Trudy hung her head and pouted.

'Come on now, Trudy,' said Dick, 'you know I would allow you to go in there if it were safe for you.'

'What about tomorrow then, Daddy?'

'We'll see.'

For most of that day, Trudy stayed in the barn, fascinated with mother and baby foal. Her mammy came out several times to check on her.

'Come on in now, Trudy, and have your tea.'

'I will, mamma, just give me a few more minutes.'

Margaret's pledge to herself was soon forgotten. Night after night she went to bed alone, and all she could think of was James. One night, when the moon was shining in the small bedroom window, she got up, and carefully listened at her husband's bedroom door for his gentle snore. She crept downstairs and out to the barn, looking back at the house, just in case.

James shot up from the hay.

'Where are you going at this time of night?'

'Nowhere,' replied Margaret. 'I came out here to be with you.'

'Jesus! No, Margaret, what are you trying to do, get me fired from here or what?'

'Not at all,' she replied. 'Why would I do that to you? You are the only friend I have around here.'

James was a lonely man. He could not resist.

'Come on over then and sit with me for a while.'

Margaret threw her arms around James and held him close. James could feel her heart beating. Her lips moved over James lips, with a passionate kiss he could not resist. Not that he wanted to. Not any more. All pretence of formality between the two of them had broken down.

After a few moments, James stopped.

'Margaret, what's going to happen? With this, I mean; with what's going on between us?'

'Nothing,' she said.

She put his hand to her breast. He held it firmly, feeling himself getting hard.

'This is me. This is real. And it's for you,' she said. 'My husband doesn't want it.'

'I do.'

'I can feel that.'

'We are taking a big risk,' said James, his heartbeat quickening.

'My husband doesn't want me. He'd rather sleep alone. So you can have me instead. Wouldn't you like to be inside me again? You want to fuck me, don't you?'

Margaret slipped out of her clothes, looking James in the eye as she did so. She knew that he was powerless to resist her. He wanted her as much as she wanted him. And she was going to have what she wanted, from one man or another.

Soon, they were making passionate love, going to heights she had never done before. She made James want her more than before, teasing him with her mouth. The second time was even better, sweeter than the first.

Margaret was elated with lovemaking. It was intoxicating. Making love in the barnyard to a man who was not her husband excited her, the wrongness of it only adding to her pleasure.

Afterwards, Margaret stayed for a while, but James was anxious, telling Margaret that he could not help himself. She comforted him by telling him that it was her fault; that if she had stayed in bed and fallen asleep like a good wife, then this would not be happening.

Margaret did not think for a moment that she would get pregnant by James. It was fun, and she considered that she deserved as much fun in her life as anybody with a decent husband would have. Perhaps foolishly, she kept telling herself that she would not become pregnant. She reassured herself that, if the worst happened, then she would somehow get her husband to do the act with her. Just the once would be enough to make everything right again, and nobody would ever need to know. She held this thought in her mind every night she left her bed and headed for the barn with James waiting.

Two months later, Margaret Fitzgerald started to worry. She kept feeling her belly and wondering. Three months came, and there was still no sign of her monthly bleed. She felt her belly swell.

She was devastated. A cold sweat came over whole body. She told James, and he nearly had a fit.

'I will kill myself,' he said. 'You must try and get rid of it.'

'How can I do that?' replied Margaret.

'I don't know,' he answered. 'Do what you have to do.'

He knew that there was nothing that he, or Margaret, could do. Margaret began to feel sick every morning. She tried to hide it from Dick and Trudy. Dick asked her on a few occasions whether she was all right. 'I'm fine,' she would answer. Dick was concerned.

'You are not eating anything at all.'

'I don't know what's wrong with me,' she replied. 'Maybe I have that awful flu that's going.'

Dick knew well what was wrong with his wife, but did not know how he was going to handle the situation. He could confront her about James, but decided to take his time and think it over. If Margaret were to leave, possibly with James, then he would be quite alone.

Six months into Margaret's pregnancy, Dick could see plain as day that his wife was with his workman's child. No matter how much as she tried to cover it up, her increasing size would no longer be concealed. Margaret continued working around the house and in the yard. She did not go to James as much now. James was just too scared, and wanted nothing more to do with her. This was one aspect of his guilt that would not be hidden in his boots. He had resolved to deny everything if confronted by his master.

Even though she was with child, Margaret still had feelings and needs. She would walk out to the yard when she knew that James was around, and make a special effort to talk to him. Margaret pleaded with James to do something. She said that he had wanted her, and now look what happened.

'I didn't really… I didn't really want you, I couldn't help it,' protested James. 'You came to me, out in the barn, that night when the foal was born. I told you then I didn't want to.'

'Didn't want to! Even if you didn't, which you did, that doesn't matter now. Now I'm in trouble, I don't know what to do. Dick won't come to my bed any more. I can't say it's his.'

James was backing away from her, pale with fear and anger.

'It's not my problem!' he shouted at Margaret. 'It's yours, and you can deal with it! I don't want to know. Keep well away from me!'

'That's not what you said when you were inside me, is it?! You unimaginable bastard!'

'You should get used to those.'

As he walked away from her, filled now with nothing but hatred, Margaret bit her lower lip, her fury mixed with fear. She remembered the nights when she had been intimate with James. Sometimes it was all she looked forward to during the day. When darkness came, she would wait for Dick to go to bed, and then out the door she would go, to where James would be waiting for her.

James could not know how Dick had turned his back when she had climbed into his bed, and how he had looked at her and told her to leave his room and from now on sleep in her own, with Trudy. It was as though she were no longer his wife. And now Margaret had tried everything she could to get Dick interested in lovemaking.

One evening, she went up the stairs in before Dick. She had a plan to be undressed and in his bed when he came up the stairs to his bedroom.

'Dick,' she pleaded, 'I want you tonight. I am feeling lonely for you. I need my husband,' she said, looking sad and forlorn.

She moved forward to put her arms around Dick, but he pushed her away coldly.

'Not now, Margaret. Not ever. I don't want any more children. Trudy is plenty for me. What has got into your head about lovemaking? Anyone would think you are some sort of a whore.'

'I'm not a whore; I'm your wife!'

'There are plenty of women in Limerick City who go out looking for love and want to get paid for it. Conduct yourself better now, or you will end up joining them.'

'I can't believe you are saying this to me.' She sobbed.

'And just because I married you, it doesn't mean you aren't a whore.'

James did not want to touch her either. Margaret was on her own, in a world that she was starting to find unforgiving. Every time she crossed the yard or went near the barn, James would vanish. She was heartbroken. A black cloud had fallen over Margaret Fitzgerald, and there was nowhere she could escape it.

When the baby began to move in her belly she would take a huge breath and pull her stomach in. Please God help me, she prayed, but her prayers were not heard. I am in an awful, wretched state, she thought, and becoming desperate. Every move from the baby was one more reminder of what was going to happen; one more reminder of inevitability.

She hated her situation, and felt unclean, and didn't know what to do about it. She knew that if she told Dick, he would probably throw her out of the house. Her parents and siblings would not want her back home with them either, as she would bring shame on them too. So Margaret had to bear her secret alone. She was terrified.

What if the baby comes during the night, what will I do, she thought to herself. I really need the nurse. How can I tell Dick? I don't know what he will do. Will he throw me out of the house? Where will I go then…?

Fear turned to outright terror as Margaret became increasingly scared, depressed and alone. She would feel the baby move every day when she woke up, then the anxiety was back, and would not release her from its grip. She would sit on the side of the bed, head in hands, and pray that she would wake up one morning to find that everything was fine again, with no baby in her belly.

Jesus have mercy on me, she would plead with God. In desperation, she began to think of how she could rid herself of this terrible burden.

Margaret did not realise that Dick already knew of her pregnancy, and was coming to the conclusion that he would not tolerate another man's baby in his house. It would be the talk of the county. What kind of a man would he be who allowed his wife's bastard child to live in his home, with its father sleeping in the barn outside? He was a failure, as a husband and as a man, and he would not allow his family's good name to be dragged into the mud. What was he thinking, marrying a young woman? He had wanted companionship; not this slut.

Dick began to detest Margaret, and he found it hard to talk to her, or to eat anything she would cook or bake for him. Sometimes he would pretend not to hear her when she asked a question. He would look at her, and her increasing size, when she was not aware.

The thought of Margaret doing what she did with James nearly drove him demented. Yet he kept silent. His only alternative was to throw the two of them out of his house forever, and he was not sure that he wanted to do that. James had been his friend for many years until this woman had arrived on the scene. No, it wasn't James' fault; it was hers, and he knew it. Dick needed help.

Chapter 10

After much thought, Dick made the decision to go to Father Henry and let him know of the situation. Deep down, he blamed the priest for encouraging him to marry Margaret in the first place. Although he was very fond of Trudy, and would keep her, he would depend on the priest to tell him what to do about Margaret and James.

The next Sunday after Mass, Dick called Father Henry aside outside the chapel gate. Father Henry suspected that something was wrong.

'Come in to the presbytery, Dick, and we'll talk.'

The priest sat Dick down, then he himself took a seat near the door. It was a cold room with no windows, just light coming in through the stained glass panel at the top of the door. There was a strong scent of incense and myrrh.

'Well, Dick, what is bothering you?' asked the priest.

'Father Henry…' Dick said, and broke off.

'Go ahead, man, I have heard it all now, nothing shocks me any more,' said the priest. 'Are you sick?'

'No, Father.' Dick replied.

'Is it Margaret then?'

Silence again. Looking at the floor, Dick began to tell of his wife's infidelity, and the consequences of it.

Father Henry's face reddened.

'My God,' he said quietly, 'that's the thanks I get, after all I did for that family, and the situation they were in. Not for one moment did I think that girl would be unfaithful to her husband. She should have been so glad she got a husband and a fine home. What possessed her to do such a thing?'

'What am I going to do now, Father? I don't want to let James go if I can help it. I can't believe that it was his fault. In my heart I know that it was her. But if I just send her away, then how is she going to manage? How is Trudy going to manage without her mother? I wouldn't know how to bring her up. I have thought of schools where they keep the children, only send them home at Christmas and Easter. Maybe she would be better off there in good hands.'

'Hold on, now,' said Father Henry, 'let's not lose the run of ourselves. We will consider all our options.'

'What options?' said Dick. 'I don't know what to do. I have been doing nothing, only thinking about the situation for the past few months.'

'How far gone is she?' asked the priest.

'I think about six or seven months, I'm not sure.'

Dick told of the night he went out to check on the mare, and what he saw.

'That must have been awful for you, Dick. I would have walked in on them both. Let them know the wrong they were up to. I would have taken a stick to that James, and given Margaret a good hiding too.'

'I was embarrassed, Father.'

'What do *you* have to be embarrassed about? *They* are the ones who should have been ashamed.'

'But if I had been a better husband for her, none of this would have happened. I did that girl a wrong, marrying her.

'You can't blame yourself for the sins of others, Dick. We only need to atone for our own wrongdoings, and those two have a lot more to atone for than you do.'

'Well there's a lot of sinning to go around; more than enough of it for all of us. If I had known what was going to happen, I would have done something. I don't know what, but something. Now… I can't see what to do. She is going to have the baby soon, and I still don't know what I'm going to do. I need help; I need advice.'

Father Henry paused for a few moments, then let out a deep breath, his eyes staring up to the ceiling for inspiration. He settled himself on the chair and leaned forward, elbows on both knees and hands clasped.

'I know what we will do, Dick. We will do what any good person would do in this situation. I will take her to the workhouse in Limerick. Leave it to me and I will make arrangements. When everything is sorted, I will come in the pony and trap and take her there. How does that sound, Dick?'

'It sounds like a nightmare. Maybe she deserves it. Maybe I do, too.'

'Dick, there is a time for thought and there is a time for action, and you need to act now. Only God can judge us for what we do; it isn't for us to judge. Nobody would judge you too harshly for acting when your situation was as serious as this.'

'All right, Father. We will do what must be done. Let me know when you will come for her, Father. And thank you.'

'It will take about a week or so to get things sorted out with the workhouse. Then that will be the end of this, and we will never need to speak of it, or her, again.'

Dick Fitzgerald depended on Father Henry for advice, and he trusted him completely. In the end, Dick was content to follow his advice. The priest, whatever else might be said about him, was a man of action, and was not given to reflect on things as Dick was prone to do. He hoped that the priest would not think too badly of him. After all, it was Father Henry who had recommended the girl in the first place. Dick thought more about the priest, and James, than he did about the fate of his wife.

★★★

Margaret Fitzgerald's favourite moments of the day were the first ones. For just a second or two when she awoke, with the sunlight playing on her face, she could feel contented. Then, after just a second or two, she would remember who she was and what she had done. As consciousness stalked her, it brought with it a feeling of dread, of guilt and of fear, and the remainder of the day would be spent trying to hide those feelings as best she could from her husband, of whom she was increasingly afraid.

Margaret had seen Dick and Father Henry walking into the presbytery, and felt sick at the thought of what they might be discussing. She tried to keep calm and show no nerves, but her hands were shaking as she felt the baby moving in her belly.

After a while, Dick came out with the priest, and Margaret knew the game was up. Dick and the priest were talking quietly, seriously, looking business-like. The business that they were discussing, of course, could only be her. A game was being played between these men, but she was not able to take part in it as any kind of player. If she was anything, which was doubtful, she was the ball.

What had she been thinking? Now, her thoughts turned to ridding herself of the baby. She wasn't sure whether she could go through with it.

Dick said nothing the entire way home. Margaret looked at him sideways, but he remained looking straight ahead, and seemed to be in another world. As they entered the laneway to home, Dick turned to Margaret.

'We will have to have a talk when we get in.'

Margaret could feel her heart drop. The blood drained from her head. She felt dizzy. She did not respond, nor did Dick wait for a reply. He tied the pony and trap at the gate, and called James to put the horse out in the field.

James' face when he saw their expressions would stop a clock. He looked bewildered, shocked, startled. In his heart, he knew that something was up. It was only a matter of time before Dick would notice his wife's growing belly.

Dick and Margaret walked into the kitchen. Margaret immediately put the kettle over the fire to make tea.

'Sit,' Dick said to her in a commanding voice from his usual chair at the end of the table. Margaret knew that the time had come. He began.

'The night the foal was born, I came into the barn to see how things were going with the mare. I saw you and James… together. I could not believe the sight. You and James. Not for a moment did I have any idea of what was happening under my own roof! I know how long this has been going on.'

He looked at Margaret, tears rolling down her face. Broken, she said nothing.

'I know the state you are in now, too. It did not take you long, did it?'

'Sorry, Dick, I never intended for this to happen. I will make it up to you,' she begged him. 'I will give the baby up for adoption, or fostering, and no one needs to know whose it is.'

Just then, she felt the baby kick, as if objecting to what Margaret was saying.

'It's too late for that now,' Dick replied. 'I will not raise or have any other raise a bastard!'

Margaret hung her head. She could say nothing more, and waited for her husband to hand down her fate.

'On Wednesday morning, Father Henry will come and collect you and take you away from here, and the good home you had. You will take nothing with you.'

'What about Trudy?' she cried.

'She will remain here with me and look after me in the years to come. She is only a child; she is incapable of looking after you, or indeed herself. I will worry about her. You go and worry about yourself. You are a disgrace to me and your own family!'

Dick stood and waited for Margaret to leave the kitchen. She pleaded and begged him to reconsider her offer of handing up the baby.

'I will not,' Dick retorted. 'How can I look that James fellow in the face again? After what he has done behind my back! The two of you should be tied together and thrown into the quarry never to get out.'

Margaret left the kitchen. She knew her husband well enough to know that it was no use pleading and begging any further.

She went upstairs to the bedroom, and cried uncontrollably. Now things were out in the open. In a way, it helped a little. She would no longer have to try and cover herself up. But she had no idea where Dick would send her, or what Father Henry would do when he collected her on Wednesday.

Margaret remained in the bedroom all that day and night. Tuesday night came, and she could not stop shuddering at the thought of the following morning.

She put a few clothes and a pair of shoes in a bag and left it on the end of the bed. Worn out, she lay down and tried to rest, but without food or a drink of water over the previous day, she felt unwell.

Margaret could have come down to the kitchen for water and food, but chose not to. She did not want to see Dick until she was leaving. She could not sleep, and the baby was uneasy in her belly. She looked around the room in desperation. Every hour seemed like a lifetime. 'It's like going to the gallows,' she said to herself out loud.

Suddenly, Margaret knew what to do. Her mind raced. She rocked backwards and forwards, her arms around her belly, feeling the world closing in on her. There was perspiration on her brow and over her top lip. She wiped it off with the sheet on the bed. After a few minutes, she calmed down. For the first time in a long time, Margaret began to think clearly....

She stood up and pulled the sheets off the bed, tied them together, then swung the sheets over the main rafter in the roof. She sat back down on the bed, picked up her prayer book and all the holy pictures she had been given by her mother. She lit the candle and prayed to the heavens to accept her, making the sign of the cross with each holy picture in her entire collection of first holy communion and confirmation medals.

Margaret thought about her parents, fretting over what they might think of her, and the choice she was now making. The embarrassment for them will be awful, especially for Mammy, she thought. I know she will miss me. She relied on me being the oldest, but now what will she do? No one can help me.... She thought about her brothers and sisters, and most of all she thought about Trudy. Poor little thing, she will miss me, but she will be better off without me.

Margaret felt a sense of relief and stillness coming over her. Even the baby in her belly was quiet. Without hesitation, slowly and methodically she climbed onto the bed again, took the sheets and made a noose. With her rosary beads in her left hand and the cross burning into the palm, she put the noose over her head and then around her neck, making sure that it was secure and tight, and swung out over the side of the bed, tipping the burning candle with her feet. This is an act of mercy, she told herself. Margaret Fitzgerald held some hope of peace at long last as she launched herself away from the bed, her husband, that priest, her child, James and everybody and everything else in this world.

The candle landed on a pile of clothes on the ground. Within seconds, the clothes were burning. Margaret swung back to the end of the bed. She was caught and held by the noose, her feet just inches from touching the bed.

Flames sprung quickly from the piled clothes. The room filled with smoke. Margaret could do nothing, suspended from the rafter in the roof, though she kicked and twisted and turned. As the bedclothes began to catch fire, the noose tightened and Margaret was slipping out of consciousness, her final thought was that she may already be in hell. She no longer had any way to tell the difference.

Within minutes, the fire was raging, its smoke thickening and rising to the ceiling. Margaret died with her unborn child from smoke inhalation, having failed to break her neck cleanly. It was not until just before Father Henry came in his pony and trap that Dick came up the stairs and saw Margaret hanging from the rafters, the room now engulfed in flames.

'No! No, what have I done!' he screamed.

Dick tried to beat back the fire with his coat, helplessly holding on to Margaret's feet, now slippery with blood and worse, trying to hold her up and provide support. There was nothing he could do; she was gone. As Dick fell back, defeated, he caught the end of the bed to steady himself. His hands was burnt by the searing heat, and nearly stuck to the hot wrought iron. He ran back downstairs for buckets of water, and managed to drench the fire, but the smoke continued hissing and spluttering.

Dick feared that the whole house would go up in flames. As fast as his legs could carry him, he ran up and down the stairs for buckets of water. In his haste to stop the flames, he tripped and spilled half the water and made the stairs slippery, yet managed to extinguish them. The danger of fire was over.

Looking at Margaret again, he felt terrified. She looked so young and miserable hanging there. It struck him that all the life was gone out of this once busy young woman who had been a fine housekeeper and a good mother to their daughter Trudy.

'God help me!' Dick cried out, sinking down to sit on the bed, and putting his head in his hands.

Outside in the yard, James wondered what was going on. He heard the commotion indoors. Perhaps Margaret's baby was arriving early. Perhaps Trudy had injured herself. When he saw the plume of smoke winding into the sky, though, he somehow knew what had happened.

Chapter 11

Bandaging his hand with a handkerchief, Dick Fitzgerald gasped for fresh air, the smoke and the shock beginning to overcome him.

James was rooted to the spot, unable to move, watching in silence. One look from Dick was enough to confirm what he already suspected.

James heard a pony and trap coming up the laneway. As it rounded the corner, he could see that it was the parish priest. Knowing nothing about the arrangement made regarding Margaret, James did his best to meet the priest. Father Henry jumped off the trap.

'Take the reins, James, and tie him to the post over there. I'll only be a few minutes.'

The priest had to have seen the smoke from miles away. He had to know. Yet Father Henry seemed, to James, oddly detached from what he was seeing.

'What's going on here?' Father Henry shouted at Dick. Dick gestured towards the bedroom.

Water was dripping down the stairs as the priest climbed them. On seeing what had happened in the bedroom, the priest went straight for the sheets, cut Margaret down and laid her on the charred bed.

He pulled out the holy oils and water from his breast pocket. He gave her the last rites and blessed her belly, then whispered the act of contrition in her ear.

'God will look after them now, Dick, we will have to decide what to do. For the moment, no one has to know anything. We can say that she died from a fall down the stairs trying to escape from the fire. When I tell her family, they won't ask any more. It's a tragedy. Give me a hand lifting her down the stairs. We will get the undertakers to come with a coffin. I will take her to the presbytery, and she can lie there until the burial.'

James was tending to the horses when he saw Father Henry and Dick taking Margaret's body out to the trap. He could not believe it. Now he dreaded his own fate. The pony and trap jogged down the laneway, and then silence, not a bush or a tree or a bird moving.

James knelt to the ground and sobbed. He knew that the only woman he had any contact with was gone from him, and he felt guilty about his own involvement in her death. Taking off his cap and throwing it on the ground, he made the sign of the cross and started praying and asking for forgiveness for this awful thing that happened. He asked God to take care of Margaret. Perhaps she could have a better time in another world than she had been granted in this one. Was it his fault? His master's? There was blame to go around, and some share in it, he knew, was his.

In a daze, he got up and entered the stables. He sat down where he and Margaret had made passionate love. He prayed for Margaret's soul, holding his rosary beads in both hands. He begged for God's forgiveness.

When Father Henry handed her body over to the undertaker, he could see that there was no mark on her neck. He wondered if it were the smoke that killed her and not the hanging, although he knew full well that Margaret intended to kill herself by hanging. He lifted his tasselled cap and scratched his head. Well, well, this is a surprise, he thought. If she did not go one way, she went another. He quickly covered her body and told the undertaker to take care of the corpse. There was no need to let Dick Fitzgerald know how his wife Margaret actually died. He was not going to inform Dick Fitzgerald of his findings. It did not matter one way or another. This woman was dead now and gone forever.

James did not know how he would carry on. His master Dick would surely sack him and banish him from Limerick. He could even take him to prison and let the law deal with him. James' past could even be brought to light....

Dick was concerned to keep the details of his wife's death a secret. Suicide was considered a sin, and the remains of those who had found their life to be unbearable would be buried outside the graveyard in the adjoining field, which would be a disgrace that would attach to a family forever, or as near to forever as the local inhabitants could manage. Dick discussed the arrangements with Father Henry. If they buried Margaret in the field, then everyone would know that she had taken her own life. If she were buried in the graveyard, though, it was going against the teachings of the Catholic Church.

'Oh God, Father, we can't bury her in that field. We can't tell her family that she ended her life like this.'

'You want her to be within the graveyard?'

'I want to save her family the pain of knowing what happened. And our daughter. It was hard enough for me to bury Catherine, my first wife. I'll buy another plot for Margaret, whatever it costs.'

'Perhaps I could find a plot for her that is out of the way,' Father Henry mulled it over. 'We have a good plot over by the wall on the left hand side. It's a bit out of the way.'

Dick could not think straight. Whatever you think, Father,' he said.

In the end, they decided to bury her in consecrated ground. She had been a devout Catholic, they reasoned, and had done no wrong, except to herself, her husband and young daughter Trudy, and her unborn child. The people whom she had left behind would not want her to be buried in a way that would not accord with her wishes.

Margaret's death was thus publicly attributed to a fall down the stairs, and nobody asked any more questions. Everyone was so sorry to see Dick Fitzgerald burying his second wife and departing the funeral with his young daughter that the whole neighbourhood were talking about this awful happening.

Many near neighbours offered their help to Dick, but he refused it. He wanted no one's help.

★★★

For a while, Dick Fitzgerald remained in a dream-like state, his daughter Trudy the only thing keeping him grounded. He could not forget the sight of Margaret hanging from the rafters. It haunted him night after night. He wished he had talked to her more, after he had told her about Father Henry coming to take her away.

Dick had nights when he did not close his eyes at all. On others, he began to sleepwalk, sometimes waking up to find himself some distance from his bedroom. Over and over, again and again, he lived through the months before her death, back to the night in the barn when he watched Margaret and James making love.

Dick could not have helped himself. Whenever he heard Margaret leave her bedroom, he would quietly go out to the barn, where he would sit in the darkness and watch.

How Margaret would laugh and throw her head back, her hair all over the place! And James, the miserable workman.... Interfering with his wife, laughing behind his back at how much older he was. How Margaret would say she needed a younger man. She seemed to enjoy herself too much, not like the woman he knew.

Dick began to feel jealous of James, and felt his own failure as a husband and a father. He blamed himself for not putting a stop to what was happening. Somehow, he thought it would keep Margaret from asking him to sleep with her. There was a streak of darkness within his soul, and it twisted his mind. He had enjoyed watching from a distance, and would feel excited as Margaret and James became more and more passionate.

He felt jealous of the passion and how they both enjoyed each other's bodies. He had never felt that way with Margaret, or his first wife Catherine.

Often, Margaret would tease James and hold on to the lovemaking until he was desperate. It excited Dick to watch it, and if he stopped them, then he would see it no more. Seeing his cheating wife being entered and degraded by another man quickened his blood in a way that few things did any more.

When they ended their lovemaking, Dick retreated quietly back into the house and up to bed. He did not sleep until he heard Margaret go back to hers.

The thoughts he used to run through, over and over again in his head when he was alone, now refused to leave him. He had nurtured them for so long, turned them over and over in the darkness of his bedroom and his mind, enjoying the time he spent within his thoughts. Now, though, they tormented him, gripping his heart and his mind, trapping him in a mental prison of his own making. He knew more than that priest did about demons. The ones to be feared were not roasting sinners in the afterlife. The ones to be feared were the ones in his mind, in his heart and in whatever he had left of a soul. The ones he had fed, and nurtured, and cared for. And now they had grown so fearsome that they would not leave him to his thoughts. There was no more silence and peace for him, for he had loved them too well.

Time, his neighbours and acquaintances were wont to say, can be a great healer. But they didn't know the truth of what had happened. Right now, he could not come to terms with it. He wanted her out of his mind, but she refused to leave it.

He began to hear noises in Margaret's bedroom on his way to bed at night. There were footsteps walking over and back to the door. I am losing my mind, Dick thought. His ear to the wooden door, he listened once again.

Nothing happened, and he turned away. Then he heard the door swing open with a whirring sound, and a mighty force that almost knocked him to the ground. Dick cried out in fear. Could the spirit of Margaret persist in the house? Startled and numb, he remained still for a few moments, then gathered himself together and got the holy water, blessed the door and the landing, all the while making the sign of the cross on his forehead. He threw some at the door and all around the stairs.

Dick remembered how his parents and neighbours would talk about the ghost or spirit of some people who had passed, and how they did not make the crossing into the next world. The person was not ready to go to the other side. Or they had died tragically, and were not yet at peace. He had done everything he could think of, covering the clocks in the house, turning the mirrors to the wall.

Dick asked Father Henry to come and say Mass in the room. Hopefully, that would settle the spirit. The priest arrived with the host in his service regalia. Serious and red-faced, he began Mass in the room, where candles were lit in each corner and a holy cross hung on the door. Only Dick Fitzgerald and the priest were in the room.

Minutes into the ceremony, Dick thought he heard a banging sound in the room. He felt afraid, wondering what he was hearing, and whether it could be her somehow, come back to torment him. Dick held his ground. The priest kept on saying Mass. Again and again, Dick thought that he heard something, a banging sound echoing through the room. If there was a spirit in there with them, then it was not a contented one. Father Henry heard nothing, or acted as if he did not, and raised his voice louder and louder, trying to convince the spirit that it was time to leave this earth and move on to the next world. Dick was terrified. He thought that all hell would break loose. All he wanted was for Margaret to rest in peace, leaving this world with his and God's blessing.

Suddenly, there was an enormous clap like thunder, and a streak of lightning shook the whole house, shattering the glass in the window. The silence that followed was as terrifying as anything that had gone before.

Father Henry finished Mass, then stayed up all night praying for the quick and safe passage of Margaret Fitzgerald's soul to the other side.

It worked. Not a sound was heard in that room again.

After Margaret's death, James did not enter the house, and stayed well away from Dick Fitzgerald, afraid of what Dick might say or do. James looked after the horses and kept the stables and barn clean. He knew that his master was grieving, but so was James. He missed the late-night passion and the company of a woman. He was not such a cruel man that he did not feel remorse for the words he had spoken in anger—words he could never take back.

Dick Fitzgerald needed almost four weeks to pull himself together. One morning, he got out of bed and decided that it was time for him to take charge of his farm and his life once again. Perhaps there was to be no salvation for him, but he would fight to give his only daughter some kind of a life without her mother. He knew that this would be a struggle, but it helped him to focus on what he had to do, and why, rather than dwelling on the wrongs of his past.

That day, he handed Trudy all the holy pictures, prayer book and holy medals.

'They're Mammy's,' she said, 'not mine.'

'Well, your Mammy is gone to heaven now, and she is not coming back here any more. So you can have them all.'

Trudy looked at her father.

'Where is she?'

'She will be away for a long time,' said Dick. He just wasn't up to explaining about death. Trudy was bewildered. She decided to go outside and think about what her father had told her.

Trudy took the prayer book, all the holy pictures, medals as well, and put them in a tin box under her bed. Every night she took them out, and one by one laid them out on the bed. She would say a prayer to each one, and pray that her mammy would come back down from heaven.

She would take the tin box to Mass every Sunday morning, and would run straight up to the front seat on the right-hand side of the chapel, and kneel down in the front pew. She would then lay out all the contents of the box on the seat in front of her and hold the prayer book in both hands and wait for Mass to start. Nobody ever joined her. It was a pitiful sight, yet oddly comforting to see the child with her holy pictures and medals.

★★★

'Steady' Eddie Malone eventually left for America, along with two other men in their twenties. First, he went home to Clonakilty to bid farewell to his parents and brothers and sisters. His mother had a little money saved, and she gave it to Eddie.

Eddie decided to call to the Fitzgeralds to bid farewell to them too, and ask after Noel and Declan. He knew that they were in Boston, but he needed their address. He couldn't forget the night he was on his way home from the rambling house, and the thought of Margaret and the workman making passionate love in the hay. Sometimes he thought he would like to be James, and other times he thought of Dick Fitzgerald and how he was being deceived by his wife. He did eventually call and spoke to Dick, asking after his sons. He told Dick that he would call on them when he got to America. Margaret was there, but he could not look her in the eye. She was in good form, however, and wished him well in America. Eddie left the Fitzgerald household with the address of the men in his pocket and an image of Margaret that he would never forget.

Dick Fitzgerald walked with Eddie down to the road gate, where the men shook hands.

'Wait a minute, Eddie,' Dick said. 'I have something very important to ask you.'

Eddie stood with his right ear towards Dick.

'What is it?' asked Eddie.

'Well, Eddie, my sons Declan and Noel…'. He paused for a second or two. 'They don't know of my second marriage to Margaret Dillon, and of course they don't know about my daughter Trudy either. They were gone to America before I remarried. I thought it best not to tell them at all, I… didn't know how they would take it.'

Eddie didn't know what to make of it. He could see that it was a heavy burden on Dick. Eddie did the honourable thing, and assured Dick that he would not mention anything about the new wife, even though he felt a bit shocked at Dick not telling his sons. In the end, though, what business was it of his whether Dick chose to tell his sons or not about his new family? Dick waved to Eddie until he was out of sight.

Back in Bruff on the Dillons' farm, he informed Mr Dillon of his plan for America. The Dillons told him that they were sorry he was going. They had a big party for Eddie and the two other young men. It was a sorry night and a happy night. Eddie had a lot to drink. The two young men he was to travel with told him that they would not put up with him drinking like that. They wanted to get to America with a clear head and look for work. Eddie promised that he wouldn't drink on the ship.

'I will be sober for the whole time,' he told them.

He couldn't wait to buy his ticket for America. The excitement of holding the one-way ticket was powerful. A one-way ticket was all that any of them imagined they would need.

The day came, and he said his goodbyes to everyone he knew. The three men headed for Queenstown with great anticipation. The rain was pouring down from the heavens, and they were soaked from head to toe. Their shoes were so wet you could hear them squelching with every step.

Boarding the ship, heading up the gangway, Eddie felt a shiver run up and down his spine. He turned to Mike.

'Someone has just walked over my grave,' he told him.

'Ah, not at all,' Mike replied. 'It's the rain going through your coat, that's all.'

Eddie was not convinced. He was worried about whether he had made the right decision, but felt that it was too late to turn back now. He did not want to look a coward in front of everyone. He soon forgot about the shiver. The excitement of the journey and the new beginning was great.

Looking back at Ireland from the sea, Eddie Malone shed a tear of both joy and sadness, rubbing it so that no one would see him. He turned around and looked forward into the horizon, to a new future that would be a rich one, or so he hoped. The thought that he might never come back to Ireland made him sad and lonely, but he did not dwell on that for too long. His travelling companions shouted at him to join them in a game of cards for one penny a man. And he did.

The voyage was long and tedious. At night, the men got together and talked, smoked and played the usual game of cards. They discussed finding work and making contact with friends that had gone before them. All of them knew someone; some had names and addresses written on pieces of paper in their pockets. Eddie knew that Declan and Noel Fitzgerald were somewhere in Boston, and he had an address in his pocket. He had got their address from Dick Fitzgerald before he left Ireland.

During daylight hours they walked around the ship, and met many others from nearby towns and counties, each man with his own private thoughts and dreams. None, however, showed emotion, preferring to put on a brave face. The tough exterior meant a lot, and somehow they felt strong together. The women were worse than the men. Many of them were missing their parents and siblings so much that they cried.

At times, the sea was rough and many passengers were sick. When the ship tilted to one side, Eddie became anxious, wondering would it ever turn upright. He was not able to swim, and so lived in terror that they were all going to drown. He had heard of a ship that had sunk in an unmerciful storm, and all the passengers were lost at sea. He said a silent prayer for their souls.

Others were not so lucky. They died of hunger and thirst. Almost every other day, someone passed away and was buried at sea. The captain would say a few words and the priest would bless the dead. Everyone on board was affected. They would count themselves fortunate indeed if they made it to America.

After six weeks at sea, they landed on Ellis Island. Queues of people all lined the wall, men, women and children. All were awaiting their turn to sign up and get clearance. The men from Bruff waited in line with the others.

There were only three officers sitting behind wooden desks with fountain-pens and ink. When you reached the officer, you had to fill out a form. Anybody who was unable to read and write, which was the majority of them, was given help. That was where many names got changed. Sometimes the officers could not hear the name properly, the 'O' prefixes often being omitted from the Irish names. Eventually, Eddie and his friends made it through. Eddie then bid them farewell, and boarded a train for Boston. His friends were to remain in New York.

On safe ground, and with a firm footing under him, Eddie had decided to go on alone. He thought that he would have a better chance of getting work without anybody else. He would work at anything he could get. When he got off the train in Boston, he walked with the hundreds of people heading home from work or going somewhere. He stood aside for a few minutes at the iron railing, lit up a cigarette and wondered where he would go to get shelter for the night.

He spotted a police officer. Eddie approached him, pulling out the name and address he had in his pocket.

'Excuse me, Officer, can you help me with this address? Sure I've just landed here in Boston and don't know how to get to it.'

The officer pointed him in the direction, telling him that it was only a ten minute walk.

'It's on the left as you get into Harper street.'

There were a lot of people walking, some in a hurry, along the same street. Eddie had never seen anything like it. There had to be hundreds of them, or thousands, all together in this place on the other side of the world.

Eventually he arrived at the address on his piece of tattered paper.

Eddie stood, knocked and waited.

Declan opened the door.

'Jesus, man, its only Steady Eddie!'

He was astonished to see his visitor. They hugged each other. Eddie was delighted.

'Any chance of a bed for the night?' he asked.

'Of course,' said Declan. 'Sure I'll put you up for the night. What's the matter with you, come in!'

The two men talked for hours. Eddie wanted to know about work, while Declan was interested in all the news from home. Eddie told Declan about who had died and who had children, and about the British soldiers coming and taking over some of the farmers' land.

Eddie couldn't get over the lovely place that the two brothers had. It was a one-bedroom flat. Noel was home already, cooking something on the stove. Eddie walked in.

'Put me in the pot there, Noel!' he shouted.

Noel turned around, and could not believe whom he was seeing.

Eddie was delighted with the welcome he was getting. He was in his element, chatting, drinking and laughing as if they had never left their homes.

'In a new world with some old friends from back home, I am.'

Eddie was drunk.

'I never thought I'd see you here, Eddie,' said Noel. 'I'm sure you're looking for work? Come with me tomorrow morning, we will leave at six a.m. I'll find out if our foreman will take you on, we always need good workers. You might be in luck.'

The men talked for most of the night, reminiscing about home. Eddie, though, wanted to talk about the future.

'Are you earning good money, lads?' he asked.

'We do okay,' Noel replied. 'We mind our money, save up and send some home when we can.'

'Do ye have girlfriends?' asked Eddie.

'No, not yet. Sure there's time enough for that, though. We keep our heads down and work hard,' said Declan.

'You haven't mentioned Bob's Mary. Is she still around Bruff?' said Noel.

'Oh, leave it so,' said Eddie. 'She is well and doing what she knows best—looking for male company! I heard that Father Henry came upon her and a big farmer one night last August. Of course, Mary only cheeked up the fecking priest! She is fit for anything, that one.'

It had been the talk of Bruff for ages. Bob's Mary continued her carry-on, attending Mass on the following Sunday with the biggest smile on her face. She did not mind that everyone knew whom she was with, and what they had been up to.

'I ran into her just before I sailed here,' Eddie told them. 'She's the same old Mary, interested in all the men around Bruff. I believe she still has the whistlers calling. She is getting a bit shook-looking through; some of her front teeth are missing, she pulls her top lip in.' They laughed. 'She looks strange, but she was in great form sure enough, wishing me well and good fortune in America. She said she had a dream once that she sailed to America, that she missed Ireland and Bruff that she couldn't fit in over here in America. When she woke in her own bed, she was relieved it was only a dream. She wanted a kiss from me. I said "Ah no, Mary, you're all right." She insisted, and made a dive on me. I was lucky, she only missed me by an inch!'

The men laughed. The time was passing more pleasantly that evening than it had in some time.

'Only for her around the place the neighbours would have no one to talk about!' said Declan.

'She keeps everyone on their toes all right,' agreed Noel. 'She knows everyone but the fecking priest!'

'Maybe him too,' Declan suggested, conspiratorially.

'That's right, lads. Maybe he was fecking jealous!'

They laughed together the kind of laughter that makes you forget all your troubles and cherish your friends. All knew, though, that tomorrow would be another day.

The next morning, Eddie Malone was taken on by the shipping company where the boys worked. He got lucky, quickly finding work as a stevedore, loading and unloading the cargoes from the constant stream of ships, working all the hours he could get. It wasn't long before he got his own place. He also tried to save and send money home to his mother. At weekends, he went to the pub and had his fill of porter and cigarettes, but he was always up and in work early on the following Monday mornings.

When Eddie became smitten, falling head over heels with his Italian girlfriend Lola, he couldn't wait to tell the Fitzgerald men, as they were his best friends. He was ecstatic about his love for Lola. She was beautiful, and smart too. Many Irish girls had come his way, and gone again. Lola was a brilliant cook, and Eddie loved Italian food. He told her there was nothing like her cooking to be had in Ireland. They married in the local church. Eddie invited all his Irish friends and comrades, and all his new friends too. Lola's family liked Eddie, and treated him like one of their own.

Whenever Eddie was not busy, his thoughts always went back to Ireland and his family in Clonakilty. Many times with a tear in his eye he shared his thoughts with Lola. He thought often about his loving mother, and how hard she had worked to keep the family fed, and about how he had worked for the Dillons. How he sent home whatever money he could. Lola wrote to his mother from time to time, and sent on small presents for his brothers and sisters. Mrs Malone was happy for her son.

'Lola is a lovely woman,' she would tell her friends. 'Eddie is the luckiest man alive.'

Eddie remained firm friends with the Fitzgerald boys, and they continued to meet up once a week and have a few drinks. The Fitzgeralds were very happy for Eddie and his new wife. The Fitzgerald men wrote home to their father, excited to tell him about Eddie Malone, and about how they had somehow met up again and remained great friends. They explained how every weekend they met up and had some beer and food together, and wrote of how they often fondly reminisced about Ireland and their home far away.

Chapter 12

Bob's Mary felt that she needed more from life. She was restless in her home, and wanted to be out and about. She was sick of cooking and baking, churning butter. Looking after her two brothers was a chore. Washing their clothes—when they bothered to change them, which was not often—did not greatly entertain her. She would complain to their ungrateful ears that she got no thanks at all for all the work she did around the home. Who else would do all of the work for them if not she? Her brothers knew her well, though, and dismissed these rants from Mary as irrelevant. A little encouragement went a long way with Mary, generally proving sufficient to send her back to what they needed her to do, and they knew how to provide such gentle nudges of encouragement in the right direction. Many of the men in the town did.

As she got older, Mary became more and more obsessed with 'men friends'. She started looking for new 'men friends' locally. She was tiring of the same faces. There some 'friends' who came for miles to visit with her, as her repute had carried for some distance on the back of a wave of gossip and chatter, little of which was sympathetic.

Bob's Mary called to the Fitzgerald household on one sunny afternoon. She knew that Dick Fitzgerald would be alone, as she had kept watch on the Sunday before. Trudy was at Fiona Meany's house, playing with her best friend.

Bob's Mary had been thinking of paying a visit to the Fitzgeralds'. She was of a mind to seduce Dick, or the workman James. Mary wanted new pastures. She was convinced that she was the greatest lover in the world, that men loved her and that women hated her out of jealousy. In this, she was not entirely mistaken. In her mind, she felt that these two men in particular needed some fiery woman to keep them company. If she was successful today, she thought they would be additions to her list of gentlemen callers.

The sun was high in the sky, and not a breeze on the trees could be heard. The day was still and bright with no clouds to be seen. An odd fly would buzz by. The birds were busy in the treetops. The usual whistlers could be heard in the distance as she left home, the warm sun on her back. She was ignoring them today.

Bob's Mary often mumbled to herself, sometimes humming a tune. Well, today was the day for a tune. She walked along without a care in the world, across the fields and down the road as far as the Fitzgerald laneway.

There was a big iron gate leading onto a winding laneway. Bob's Mary just took a running jump and swung her long legs over the gate, not a bother to her. She picked up a piece of grass and put it between her lips, where it dangled from her mouth. She wandered slowly up the lane. As she rounded the corner on the lane, she stood gazing at Dick Fitzgerald's fine house. Her step light, she walked up to the door, where she stood with her head and body sideways and her ear to the door, listening for any voices or movement in the house. She heard Dick walking around the kitchen, then gave a big knock on the door and walked in.

Startled, Dick turned around.

'Who is that?'

'It's me. Mary,' she replied.

'What business do you have coming here?'

'Ah, Dick,' she smiled, 'I only came to see you and ask about your health. I thought you would be lonely too. Would you like my company for a few hours? We could sit together in that grand big chair you have at the fireside. Wouldn't the two of us sit comfortable in it so?'

Dick looked over at the chair.

'What are you talking about, woman? I am not going to sit with you anywhere. Go on home with yourself now, like a good woman.'

'No man has ever refused me,' Mary replied. 'I make it worth their while to sit with me. Who do you think you are? Do you think you are too good for me? Well, I am a respectable farmer. I have almost as many acres as you, Dick Fitzgerald.'

'Well, this man will not entertain you, Bob's Mary. I am sure you have plenty of local men to do just that.'

'It's you I want, Dick, not any other. Have you lost your faloorum? Have you nothing in your trousers for a woman?'

She took the sweeping brush in hand and started to sweep the floor.

'Jesus, woman. Put that brush down and leave it there where it was.'

'No!'

Bob's Mary was stubborn, and would not put the brush back. Instead, she pulled her skirt up over her head.

'Oh my God,' said Dick. 'Put that skirt down or you will frighten my dog.'

'Come on, Dick, how can you refuse a fine woman like me? Take the chance, you would be a happy man after I am finished with you. I can make you happy every day, and you don't have to come and whistle for me. I will come when I know things are quiet around here.'

'Get out, Mary, and don't come back ever again!' Dick shouted.

But Bob's Mary sat down on the chair by the fire and was silent. Dick didn't know what to do next, so he waited.

'Have you nothing to do or say to me?' asked Mary.

She just stared straight ahead, pouting. Dick stood looking at her. He did nothing, so she eventually stood up and pulled down her skirt.

'Dick Fitzgerald,' she said, 'you will be sorry you refused me.'

'I've refused better women than you, Mary, and there are many of them. Now please leave my house.'

Mary did not leave the Fitzgeralds' yard before visiting James in the stables. She pushed the barn door open with her stick.

'James, come out from your hiding place, I'm waiting for you!'

She was angry. James emerged from the dim light of the stable.

'Come on over here, with me.' Bob's Mary fixed some hay for them to sit on. James smiled at her.

'What are you doing coming here? If the master sees you, he will hunt you off the property.'

'Don't worry about that,' she said, 'I have been talking to him myself. He knows I'm here. Actually, he sent me out here to you. He said you needed company for the evening.'

James took a deep breath in, and let it out slowly.

'He never said that. I know him too well,' he replied.

'Well, I don't give a shite,' she replied, 'I need a man and I need him now. I'm on feckin' fire here.'

She watched his reaction, and then delivered the crucial blow.

'If you don't do what I want, I will tell everyone about you and Margaret Fitzgerald.'

The knowing smirk on James' face did not survive this.

'That's right; I saw you two up to your tricks in the barn here. Liked it rough, did she? One night while I was walking home, I heard the shouts and screams and laughing, I peeped in the door and there you were, the two of you.'

'What do you want with me? You have more farmers to plough you than these fuckin' fields do.'

'Now there's no need to be rude, is there? And no, I don't have as many gentlemen friends as I once did, on account of me teeth. Besides, I wonder whether your master would be interested to know about what I saw.'

'He wouldn't believe you.'

'Oh really? You want to bet, do you? I won't just be telling him, oh no. I will tell everyone about what I saw going on here before she died, and how you got her in the family way. You think he doesn't know whose babby she was carryin'? I will tell Dick, and you will be fired. Now shut the feck up and do what I want you to.'

There was an element of conjecture in this, but Bob's Mary knew of what she spoke. She certainly knew enough things about enough people to make most men a little afraid of her. There had been a lot of talk at the time Margaret died. Now, she was content to imply to James that she knew everything.

James stood like a frightened rabbit caught in a snare. As his thoughts twisted, it tightened.

'Come on now, James, are you a man or a mouse? I'll let you know when you've finished.'

He could not refuse.

Bob's Mary walked up to him until her breasts pushed against his chest. Pushing him to his knees, she lifted her skirt.

'You are a vile woman, Mary, vile.'

'Don't worry, I'll let you know when you've finished so.'

As she said this, she pressed his face into her and began to moan.

'Come on now, you are not a boy any more,' said Mary. She moaned and groaned, throwing her head back. 'You're my man, James, you are, oh, you are…'.

Moments later, James pulled her onto the floor and had her in a way that did not require that he looked at her misshapen face. Then it was over, almost before it began.

Bob's Mary stood up, brushed herself off and gave James a few slaps around the ear and a kick in the leg.

'Sure you'll do better the next time. You are in too much of a hurry to get finished. You are like a boy. I'll make you the best lover around here, wait and see.'

'I don't want to be your lover!' said James hoarsely.

'What are you on about, James?' she said. 'You should be delighted with me. I am the finest woman around here, am I not? Who says I want a lover? I am not looking for anyone.'

'You can go now, Mary,' said James, 'before the boss comes out to check the horses.'

'In my own good time,' she replied, brushing the hair back out of her sweat-covered face.

She slowly walked out, giving a little cough along the way. James fell back on the hay, his head in a spin. He knew that she would be back.

The next Sunday, he went walking, hoping not to meet Bob's Mary on the road. Whenever he heard a whistle in the distance, he knew that she was occupied, and probably wouldn't come looking for him. In the end, though, there was little that he could do to avoid her. She would come looking for him, and would find him sooner or later.

Sure enough, just a couple of weeks later on a Sunday she strode into the barn as if she owned the place, a stick in her hand. She stopped in the doorway of the stables.

'Come on now, James, are you ready for me? Your beautiful woman is here to see you, the finest lover in all the land so.'

James peeked out from behind the hay like a shy little boy.

She shouted again, 'Come out of there, I am coming after you, you eejit!'

Out James crept, like a lamb to the slaughter.

Bob's Mary left the stables with a smile on her face, or as near as she could manage.

'Sure I'll be back soon,' she informed James.

'Don't be in any hurry back here. Take your time,' James replied.

James was in a state of shock for a while after she left. His head was in a spin again. What am I going to do with this one? he wondered to himself. Perhaps she would find a more interesting target for her affections before too long. But what if she didn't? The prospect of regular visits from Bob's Mary did nothing to improve James' state of mind. He was stuck, blackmailed, and it was his own stupidity that had got him into this situation.

As it happened, Bob's Mary did not return to James that year.

That evening, Anna Meany, Trudy's godmother, walked Trudy home. Bob's Mary came down the lane and met the two girls. She looked cross.

'Where are you two going?' she said.

Anna replied that she was only walking Trudy home.

Bob's Mary looked at Anna with new interest. 'What age are you?' she asked her.

'I am eighteen years old,' Anna replied.

'You are becoming a fine young woman,' said Bob's Mary. 'Have you ever had a boyfriend?'

'No,' Anna replied.

'Are you interested in men at all?' the older woman asked.

'I would hope to marry someday, when the right man comes along.'

'I can introduce you to lots of men, if you like.'

'Ah no,' said Anna.

'All right so,' Bob's Mary replied.

Anna thought about the offer for the next week. She called on Bob's Mary on Sunday afternoon.

'Well, Miss Meany,' Bob's Mary said when she saw Anna, 'I suppose you are looking for a man? Does your mother know you are here with me?'

'No,' Anna replied, 'she does not know, and I will not tell her either.'

Anna became shy when Mary asked her about sex, and whether she had done it before.

'No, never,' she told her.

'Let me think,' said Bob's Mary. 'Who would be the right man for you?' Anna became flustered. She said that she had to go home again, that she forgot she had to mind the young children for her mother.

'Maybe I will come back next Sunday,' she said, red-faced.

'You are only making that up,' said Bob's Mary. 'You came here to meet someone, and now you just want to go home! You are useless.'

'I will come again,' Anna replied, and she ran out the door and down the lane as fast as her feet would carry her.

When she got home, she went straight to the bedroom and lay down. Her mother called to her.

'What's wrong with you, Anna? You look like a ghost! Was someone following you home or what?'

'No, Mammy, I'm all right. No one was following me at all.'

What was I thinking? she thought. If Mammy finds out, she will kill me. Bob's Mary has lost her mind, if she ever had one to lose.

Now Anna was afraid that Bob's Mary would pursue her again to go with men. Anna wanted to, but was too afraid of those older men. Bob's Mary later visited the Meany household, enquiring about Anna and if she was ready to meet men friends. Mrs Meany was shocked, and told her to get out and take all the men for herself, if she hadn't already.

Bob's Mary then tried to convince Anna's mother to agree to meet men. Mrs Meany told Bob's Mary that Father Henry had found a suitor for Anna, and that she would marry soon. Bob's Mary mumbled to herself and walked out the door. She shouted back over her shoulder.

'I don't believe you. No one will marry her. She's not fit for anyone! What man would want a wife who lived on the side of the road and had nothing? The men around here would want better than that. She has no hope of marrying anyone.'

Mrs Meany, usually a calm and sedate woman, leapt up from her chair in fury and was out the door behind Mary.

'Hold on a minute, "Bob's" Mary. Everyone knows what you are up to, and it's not for young girls like my Anna, you mangy old bag. You think you are a great one, but you are nothing but a slut.'

Bob's Mary turned around to face Mrs Meany. With one swipe of her hand, she knocked Mrs Meany to the ground, shouting, 'Get away from me! I won't let anyone talk to me like this. Your husband is no good to work; all he's good for is making babies. Don't you have enough babies? More than you can feed and clothe!'

Mrs Meany stumbled to her feet. She clawed at Bob's Mary, who ducked, and poor Mrs Meany fell again. This time, Mary jumped on top of her and pulled her hair and spat in her face.

'I'll give you a real fight!' Mary snarled. She held Mrs Meany down for a few seconds. 'Be quiet now!' Bob's Mary shouted at her.

The next thing, Mr Meany appeared, stooping, at the door. He had heard the commotion from the bedroom, where he was taking one of his many naps. He pulled the two women from each other.

'Jesus Christ, what's going on here?! Get out of here, Mary, or God help me I'll get you out.'

'A miracle! He can walk! See, I can get your husband moving even if you can't!' She spat on the floor, and that done, she was gone.

Ben Meany helped his wife to her feet. She was in a state of shock. Bob's Mary left the house with her usual swagger undiminished.

Mr Meany berated his wife for taking on Bob's Mary.

'You are no match for that bitch,' he said. 'What were you thinking?'

'She was saying things about our Anna, that she was not good enough for any man around here,' protested his wife.

'Come on, now' he said. 'Sit down and I will make you a cup of tea.'

Mrs Meany was very shaken for a few days after the fight. She warned her daughter not to have anything to do with her ever again.

Chapter 13

Mrs Meany didn't know what to do. She thought about going to Father Henry and asking him to have a word with Bob's Mary, to stop Bob's Mary bothering Anna, but that would bring trouble on them, and so Mrs Meany decided that she would go to Mr Kenny, the Headmaster in the school, and tell him what happened and ask for his advice.

The following week, she went to the school and asked for him. Mr Kenny greeted her in a kind and friendly manner. He thought that she wanted to know how her children were getting on with the schoolwork. Mrs Meany complimented the master on his good work for all the children in the neighbourhood. She then explained the reason for her visit, telling him how Bob's Mary had been bothering her eldest daughter Anna.

'I don't know what to do about this,' she exclaimed.

The master told her not to worry, she was harmless really. Bob's Mary would find herself another man, and that would keep her occupied for another while anyway.

The Master informed Mrs Meany in confidence that he too had had an encounter or two with Bob's Mary. On her way home from town one day, just as school was over, she pulled into the schoolyard, tied the donkey and cart to the tree and walked in, as brazen as you like.

'I thought she had drunk porter, but there was no smell off her breath, just the tobacco,' he told Mrs Meany. 'I was correcting the children's homework, and in she came with the biggest smile on her face. "Hello, Sir," she said, "how are things with you and your wife?" "We are very well, thank you." She asked, "You have no family do you?" I told her no, that we are not blessed with children. Then she wanted to know, "How come you don't have children? Are you not able to do the thing that makes them?" "That's not a nice thing to ask anyone," I told her,' he said. Mrs Meany was shocked, and then even more shocked.

'Then she said, "Well, I am available to teach you. Have you time now? We could make a start." I told her to stop that talk. What would my wife think of it? To that, Mary said, "Go on now, I won't tell her if you don't. I could make you happy for a while. I am not in a hurry home today."

'I told her no thanks, that I was busy with my papers there, and I didn't and I wouldn't have time to be doing that kind of thing, that I am a married man with a responsible job. "Lots of men are," she said, "but they still enjoy their time with me." I told her no, and turned my back and began to write on the blackboard. Mary was quiet until I turned around, and there she was with her skirt pulled up to her waist. "What do you think of this?" she said. I told her, "For God's sake, Mary, stop this carry on. This is a school and I am the master. If anyone saw what you were doing, Father Henry would excommunicate you from the church." "I don't know what that is," she said.

'So I explained to her that she would not be able to go to Mass any more, and then what would she do? She said, "Ah, I don't give two fucks about him, I'll go to Mass anyway. Sure he won't see me at the back of the chapel. He is always happy when I put money on the plate during the collection." She said that anyway, when she goes to confession she confesses everything, that Father Henry likes the stories and sins she has to tell him, and he never gives out to her and only gives her three Our Fathers to say for her penance. She said that he gives her absolution, and sure she has no sins then.

'After that, I left the classroom and Mary eventually left. I was watching from my house. My wife wanted to know what the problem was, so I told her. She was embarrassed for me.'

Mrs Meany felt awful for the master. Such men should not have to deal with the likes of Bob's Mary.

'That woman should be locked up,' she said. 'Lord, Sir, look at what you had to put up with.'

The Master also said that he would try and find work for Anna, and that his wife might have some housework for her.

'Anna would be better off occupied. She is a good young woman,' he told Mrs Meany. 'She was an interested student at school. If she would like a reference, I will give her one.'

Mrs Meany went home happier than she was when she arrived. The thought of getting work from Mrs Kenny made a difference. She had many other worries about her children.

Her husband Ben had no work. He had worked for a big farmer, John Ruth, nearby, until the farmer had him ride the horse one frosty morning when the fog was coming down thick and fast. Ben could not see where he was going. The horse got startled, and jumped into the quarry. Ben was thrown down into the water at the bottom of the quarry. He landed heavily on a rock sticking out of the water. He could not get up. The horse bolted and returned home. It was not until afternoon that the Ruth family came looking for him. They had to make up a kind of stretcher to put him on while they carried him out of the quarry. They took him to hospital, where he stayed for three months. He had a bad back injury, and some cuts and bruises that took a long time to heal.

The Ruth family were very kind to Ben and Mary Meany and family. They brought them meat and vegetables each week, and kept them fed. They also paid for his hospital stay, John Ruth felt it his responsibility to look after his employee. He was kind-hearted, and couldn't see the Meany family hungry. He went above and beyond the call of duty for the Meanys. When Ben came home after the hospital, they continued to take care of the family until John Ruth died, when the food supplies stopped.

Ben never worked again. He developed arthritis in his spine, and spent most of his time in bed. He felt more comfortable in bed as the pain was not as severe. The pain he lived with, however, did not prevent him from making more children. He was of little help to his wife as she looked after him, washing and shaving him and cutting his hair. She would often say that he was worse than a child. He was able to make it into Limerick city every now and again to have a glass of porter. Mrs Meany was perhaps too kind to him. He should have been up out of bed and helping her with the children. He was too fond of himself, though, and was more than content to spend his time in bed, being waited on by a struggling wife.

Ben Meany's children would tease him about his condition, imploring with him to get out of bed and join them. He would get angry and shout at them to go away. Mrs Meany would have to step in and tell them to leave daddy alone as he was very sick and had to stay in bed and they were not to torment him. In truth, they were sick of him lying in bed all the time. He looked lazy and rough.

When he did get up out of bed, all he did was complain about the noise in the house and the fact that they had no food. He would sit by the fire, dispensing orders like a general to his family of footsoldiers.

Anna started to work for the wife of Mr Kenny, the local schoolmaster. Now and again, she would run into Bob's Mary. Bob's Mary would not look at the side of the road that Anna was on. Anna was delighted that Bob's Mary did not want to talk to her, and kept her eyes cast down.

Even with her daughter's employment, the death of John Ruth, and the cessation of their main supply of food, meant that Mary Meany was struggling to get from one day to the next. Her daughters Anna and Aoife were unmarried, and like many other young women began to see their prospects as being brighter overseas. They began speaking of moving to America, Canada or Australia. There, they hoped, they would be able to find husbands and work, and might be able to send some money back home. They settled on Canada.

Mary Meany could do nothing to stop them. Although it saddened her to see her daughters planning to leave, the truth was that there was nothing else for it. Life had little to offer them if they stayed at home, and some part of Mary was happy to see them getting away, getting out of this place once and for all.

This required money, and they had none. With all the dignity she could muster, Mary asked the Kennys for their help. The schoolmaster agreed to loan them the money they needed for the trip, giving the fare to the two sisters on the proviso that they would return the money on receipt of their first pay packet in Canada. They trusted the girls to do the right thing.

Mrs Meany and the other children were all saddened to see the two sisters going away together to a foreign land.

Mary knew that she would probably never see them again. Letting them go was the hardest thing she had ever done. But for her lazy husband, they would have been able to stay with her. This was his fault, she felt, and she cursed the day she had married this feckless, idle man. His idleness had sent her daughters away from her, and for that she would never forgive him.

Six months later, the Kennys received a letter from Anna and her sister. The two girls were as good as their word, and the letter contained all of the money that was owed. Mrs Kenny went to Mrs Meany and told her of the good news. The girls had made the long trip safely, were working and were both well.

Mrs Meany was also delighted to receive a letter with quite a substantial amount of money for her and the rest of the family. Three more of the Meany family had followed Anna and Aoife to Canada, where their sisters looked after them with great care and found work for them.

Over time, the friendship between Mrs Meany and the Kennys flourished. Seeing the hardship that she was suffering, they asked her if she would be interested in a few days' work for them, just like Anna had done before. Mrs Meany was over the moon about working for the Kennys. She started early each morning, walking with the children when it was time for them to go to school. It was a new life for her. She loved working for the Kennys, and they in turn gave her food and clothes for the children. The Kennys also helped Mrs Meany with her reading and writing.

Mr Kenny coached Mrs Meany in reading and writing when she had finished the housework. Over time, she improved.

When a letter from Canada would arrive, she would bring it to the Kennys and have them read it aloud. Then the master would get her to practice reading it herself. She was afraid that she might get it wrong, and wanted to hear it from them first. Mr Kenny encouraged Mary Meany with her reading, correcting her errors, and resisting any urge to be critical of her efforts. Over time, she developed into a more confident reader. She remained nervous, but her confidence with written words steadily developed.

Mr Kenny and Mrs Meany would discuss the letters in depth. Mrs Meany would revel in her daughters' accomplishments, saying how proud she was of her girls. They had managed to make the journey on the ship, leaving home and going into the unknown, foreign country. She was amazed at their resourcefulness, as well as their kindness in sending money to her and the other children. The master was full of praise too. He was very happy for the girls and their achievement. He complimented Mrs Meany on how she had reared her children.

'Ah, Sir,' she said, 'I did the best I could with what little I had. I brought them up to be good Catholics, and to remember their religion and their homeland.'

The master assured her that he knew they were good girls and would do well.

The girls also wrote about where they were living, and what their home was like. It was part of a big block of a type that Mary had never seen, with over one hundred and fifty of what they called apartments, some with one bedroom and a small kitchen and living area. The girls had two bedrooms and shared a bathroom down the hall. They had a table with four chairs in the kitchen, and a gas cooker, which they used in the evenings. They had comfortable beds with lovely bedclothes, a wardrobe to hang their clothes in, and a chest of drawers. In their living-room they had a couch and two armchairs covered with flowery fabric of green and red colours. They even had a flush toilet in the shared bathroom, which was just about unimaginable in Bruff.

'Wouldn't it be grand, Sir, if we had that here in Ireland? Aren't they so lucky, Sir, to have that kind of living?'

'I see students come and go with the years, and it's often the ones who work hardest who turn out to be the luckiest.'

'I miss them all so much. I wish that life here could be better, so they never had to leave.'

'I know that. I know...'.

The girls were working together in a pottery factory, where they packed the pottery for shipment and worked in the canteen, and the youngest, Mary, got a job in the office answering the post. Mrs Meany would imagine them coming home from work, cooking their food and doing the housework.

'They are all grown up now,' the master said, 'and fine young women.'

'Thank you, Sir. You are very kind to me and my family. I don't know what we would do without you,' Mrs Meany replied.

But she missed her daughters, and was hopeful that they would return for a holiday someday. She told Mr Kenny that when she went to bed at night she could imagine the girls having a good life in Canada. She thought about going to join them herself, but that would mean bringing Ben with her. She wasn't so sure about that.

Mary's younger girls were with her still, and she made the time to sit with them at the kitchen table, reading schoolbooks and writing essays. It was teamwork, which the children enjoyed too.

The master could see a marked improvement in the Meany children. It gave him an idea: he would ask all the mothers to participate in their children's homework. To try and involve the mothers more in the education of their children seemed like a great idea. Those mothers who were unable to read themselves, which was many of them, could be taught alongside their children, learning to read and write together. Sadly, many of the mothers said that they were too busy to be sitting down with their children's work. They were not interested. The mothers who did, however, benefited from the homework and working with their children. For them, being able to read the local paper, or sign a document for themselves, was enough to change the world.

Chapter 14

Dick Fitzgerald was very proud of his little girl. He did everything he could to accommodate her, especially with her education. Somehow, he knew that she would be independent, and felt that he could depend on her in the years to come. Trudy was the brightest and most intelligent child in the school. She soaked up all the knowledge she could from the books the schoolmaster would lend her, and was also fluent in both Irish and English by the age of six.

'I hope I am around when you are all grown up,' Dick would say to her sometimes.

'You'd better be,' she would reply.

Dick began to think about how he would give her all he had. He really wanted her to travel and see the world; something he had done himself to some extent when he was a young man with no demands on him. The Ireland he had known, though, was disappearing before his eyes, bit by bit, the rule of foreign landlords and their agents doing nothing to help what was becoming a desperate situation. He wanted better for Trudy, and could see that she too would do better to leave Ireland and find herself a new home elsewhere.

Dick did not, however, relish the prospect of being alone in his old age. If he were to be left all alone with nothing but an empty farm and his memories, his life would be wretched indeed. He felt torn between these possibilities, and was unsure what would be for the best.

He did not give any particular thought to James—he was only there to work and tend to the horses. What was once a close friendship was now decidedly cold. He never entirely blamed James for the death of his wife, but neither did he choose to spend time with him in the way that he had done in the past.

Dick also considered asking the schoolmaster to take in Trudy during the school week, sending her back home at weekends. It was the only thing he could come up with for his daughter. He had read in the newspaper about a boarding school that was being built in Limerick City, which would be ready the following year. This new school would be run by nuns, and the children who attended it would stay at the school, coming home only at Christmas and Easter and for the summer holidays. It would be very expensive to board a child. It sounded ideal for Trudy, but Dick decided that he would try the local school and the headmaster first. He dressed himself in his best clothes, and went to see the schoolmaster, who lived in a house adjoining the school.

The master always wore a pin-stripe suit without a collar on his shirt, just a stud at the neck. Pale-skinned, with a big head of white hair, he walked with his head held to the right-hand side. He smoked a crooked-stem pipe. His wife was a very good-looking, petite woman, and dressed fashionably. She wore her hair in a bun at the nape of her neck. She had a lovely smile, and welcomed everyone who knocked at her door.

'Come in,' she said to Dick, smiling. He followed her into the long, narrow parlour, with windows at each side. 'Please take a seat, Mr Fitzgerald. Is it the master you are looking for?'

'If you don't mind, Missus, there is something I would like to discuss with him.'

She left, and soon after the master entered with a welcoming smile. Dick stood to shake hands. Everyone in the townland respected the teacher, and depended on him to educate their children, as well as help with paperwork of any kind, anything from reading a letter to writing a will.

Dick Fitzgerald laid out the proposition regarding his daughter Trudy to him, and offered a fee for the service if he accepted. The schoolmaster said that he would agree to keep Trudy and look after her during the week. He asked Dick for money for books and writing materials. Trudy was a very bright young girl, and would do very well in school. The master would not have done this for any child; he could see that Trudy needed someone to take care of her. He was a kind man with no children of his own, and unlikely ever to have any. He reassured Dick that Trudy would do well with him and his wife; she would be fed, washed, and receive extra tuition in the evenings. She would have a clean bed in a room of her own.

Dick came away from the master very satisfied with the meeting, in the knowledge that his daughter would get a decent education, yet he could not help remembering her mother, and the manner of her death. If things had not gone the way they did, Trudy would still have her mother to take care of her and take her to school and look after her. Whatever else Dick Fitzgerald could do, he could never replace the little girl's mother.

Trudy dwelt on this less than her father did. She did not know any better. Although Dick felt satisfied that he was doing the right thing for his daughter, he still felt sorrow mixed with the sense of satisfaction. The image of Margaret hanging from the rafter in a burning room in what had once been their home together tormented him, and thoughts of Trudy led to thoughts of her. All the way home in the horse and trap he thought of nothing else.

In desperation he looked skyward. 'Jesus help me,' he pleaded, not for the first time.

He met Trudy on the lane into the house.

'Where are you going, Trudy?' he asked.

'Nowhere at all, Dad. I was waiting for you to come home. I was worried; you were gone a long time.'

He pulled the pony up, and she climbed up beside him. He began to tell her of his meeting with the schoolmaster. When he was finished, she said, 'Well, I want to come home every Friday evening, and I am not going back until Monday morning.'

A confused Trudy looked at her father.

'What will you do with me when I get holidays from school?'

'You will stay at home, of course.'

Trudy didn't know what to think of this new arrangement with the schoolmaster and his wife. She tossed and turned for most of the night. In the end, she fell into a deep sleep and dreamed about her mother. In the dream, she told her about the new arrangement that her Daddy had made.

In the dream, her mother told her that she would be fine, and bent down and kissed Trudy on the cheek. She wanted Trudy to have a good life, and had every confidence in her. She also said that she had a vision of Trudy sailing off on a ship to a land far away, and that she would be a very rich and influential woman one day. Her mother would be so proud of her. She also whispered that Trudy must not let anything stop her from making the decision to leave Ireland. Trudy would go where no woman had ever gone before, Margaret said in the dream.

'Have confidence in yourself, Trudy. Never doubt yourself. Don't be afraid.'

Still sleeping, Trudy watched her mother leave through the bedroom door, smiling and waving. This dream was of some comfort, as all she wanted was to feel welcome in the new house.

That next Monday morning, James prepared the pony and trap for Dick Fitzgerald to bring Trudy to the schoolmaster's house, where she would meet the schoolmaster's wife.

Trudy hopped up onto the trap and they headed down the lane.

'Stop, Daddy,' she cried out suddenly, 'I have forgotten something!'

'What is it now, Trudy? You have everything, haven't you?'

'Everything but my prayer book and medals, I can't go without them.'

Trudy ran back to the house and up the stairs, grabbing her tin box with all the medals and holy pictures.

When the first day at school was over, Trudy went into the master's house, where Mrs Kenny was waiting for her.

'Welcome, child' she said, her arms outstretched.

After dinner, Mrs Kenny asked Trudy if she could play cards.

'Not very well at all,' Trudy answered ruefully. 'My dad plays with his friends sometimes when they come to our house. I was never allowed to stay up and watch them.'

'Well now, I will teach you to play whist, and other games too. Let's sit down over here at the card table,' said Mrs Kenny.

The small, round table had a green cover on it and a pack of cards in the middle. Within weeks, Trudy could play as well as Mrs Kenny, so she allowed Trudy to participate in a game of whist with some of her women friends.

Trudy and Fiona Meany became the best of friends. They sat together in school, ate their lunch together and on Fridays walked home from school together. Fiona depended a lot on Trudy to help with her school lessons. Fiona would ask Trudy why she couldn't come home every evening with all the other children.

'I'm staying with the master and his wife. My father has made arrangements for me.' Trudy would tell her. 'I will be at home for the summer holidays and we can meet and play all day if you like.'

During the summer holidays, Trudy looked forward to Fiona coming to visit and play. One particular Monday, it was raining all day. Trudy was alone in her bedroom, laying out her holy pictures and medals. She wished that Fiona would come to play. She was reciting the rosary out loud in the room, her holy pictures laid out on the bed, when she heard the gate to the yard open, and looked out the window, and there was Fiona coming to visit.

When Trudy went home at the weekends, her dog Miller would wait for her halfway down the lane. Dad would sit in his usual spot in the kitchen.

'Tell me everything that went on all week,' he would ask her.

'Well, Dad, I did everything I was asked. After school, the master teaches me more, and tells me everything I want to know. He knows everything.'

'What about Mrs Kenny?' he asked.

'Oh, she is very nice, and kind. She is so kind to me. Gives me lovely dinners, and I get breakfast too. Then, when her friends come to visit, they play cards, and they let me play too, because Mrs Kenny taught me. Will we have a game later, Dad?'

'I don't remember where our playing-cards have gone, Trudy.'

'I will go and look for them,' she said. 'Will you play if I find them?'

'Of course I will, Trudy. Then I can see how good you are.'

That night, by the glowing fire and the odd spark flying, Trudy asked her father to have a game of cards.

'Well, Trudy,' he replied, 'I would prefer chess. Did they teach you that? There are a few things your dad can teach you too. I'll show you how to play.'

'Yes, let's. Wait till I show the master that I can play chess, he won't believe it!'

'It' been quiet a while since I had the chessboard down on the table.'

Dick rummaged around for the chessboard, eventually finding it at the back of the dresser. Some of the pieces had seen better days. He explained each piece and how the game worked. Trudy could not take it all in.

'I can't remember it all. How does this piece move?'

'Have patience, Trudy,' he said. 'It takes a bit of time to learn it all, but I know you can do it. It's a great game once you get to know it.'

She got to know it, of course. Before the evening was over, Dick's was struggling to defend his king from his young opponent's attack. The child moved her pieces with purpose, and the game was getting away from him. His queen was no longer on the board, his king unable to castle to safety.

Trudy would have happily played all night long, but with the fire dying down and the house getting cold, Dick was ready to call it a night.

'It's not over yet, we have to finish the game.'

She was persistent.

'Tomorrow night, Dad, we'll do the same. I love playing,' she told him.

As he studied the board before going to his bedroom, Dick saw that his pieces had been pinned down and trapped.

He was hardly able to move. Wherever he looked, he saw the possibility of attacks, with few resources available to defend a position that was falling apart.

★★★

The schoolmaster and his wife grew fond of Trudy, and encouraged her to stay with them at weekends occasionally. They took her into Limerick City. She had never been there before, and was mesmerised with all the people and houses and shops. She wanted to look at the globe when she got home. Even so, she got lonely, missing her dad, Miller the dog and her own bedroom.

Trudy got on so well with the extra help from the master that she was soon far ahead of her classmates. He had to act, and it seemed wrong to stop teaching her for the benefit of the others. The answer was plain: Trudy would be his assistant. He told her that she was more than able to take over the history and geography class the following week.

'That will give me a break for an hour or two,' he said.

Trudy was not a bit fazed.

'Please, Sir, what page do we begin with the geography and history lesson?'

'Carry on from where I stopped last Friday.'

Trudy spent that weekend reading both books; she wanted to know everything first hand and then have the confidence to stand up behind the master's desk.

Her classmates laughed at her, shouting when she tried to start, and making noise with everything they had in their hands. But Trudy walloped the stick on the master's desk, and they all stopped, surprised.

'Open your books, and don't waste time, or you will never learn. And then you won't know any history or geography.'

'Who are you to teach us, Trudy Fitzgerald?'

Trudy, though, remained resolute.

'I am going to get the master if you don't stop.'

Then there was silence. Trudy began teaching her first class at nine years of age. The master had confidence in her ability, so every week Trudy would take over those two classes. She drew on her imagination and ingenuity to make it interesting for her classmates. The children began to call her Miss Fitzgerald. Trudy liked that. It made her feel in control of the class.

In the evenings, the master would coach Trudy on how to get the lesson across to her classmates and plan the curriculum for the next day. When the school inspector was expected for his annual visit, everything would be changed back to the correct curriculum, as the master would have a month's notice of his arrival. This also gave him plenty of time to clean up the classroom and the yard outside.

Chapter 15

Mary Meany was grateful that her daughters were sending her money every month. It had made a difference in her life, as had her growing abilities to read and write. She had struggled long and hard, and was gradually becoming a different person.

It was with great joy she would walk out to the postman in the morning, knowing what she would find. Opening the letters and being able to read them without assistance provided her with joy of a kind that not everybody would understand.

She had enough money to buy new clothes for her remaining small sons and daughters, and still had enough to put food on the table.

Ben, however, was not so sure about the merits of the changes in his wife, though he was more than happy with the increase in funds, providing, as it did, extra food in the house.

Mrs Meany would begin to put away a little for a rainy day, then a little more, then just more. She did not know why she did what she did, but she was beginning, bit by bit, to distrust the wisdom of her husband.

She continued to work for the Kennys, and kept her reading and writing going. She improved so much that the master suggested that she should help other mothers in her situation, giving them reading and writing lessons after school.

'Who would want lessons from me, Sir? Sure they'd think me a fool. I'm not long able to read and write myself.'

'Take your time, Mary. You're already more confident than you used to be. You're a different person. Reading lights up the world, don't you find?'

'It does. And I can't thank you enough for all your help, Sir.'

'Think about it, Mary. You could thank me by helping others to learn. You would be doing a very good thing indeed. If you teach just a few people, and each of them teaches just a few more, then before long there could be a lot of people whose lives we might be able to change for the better.'

She was nervous about the prospect, but she nodded in agreement.

As she made her way to her home and her husband, Mary Meany reflected. Perhaps she could help other people to read. But then, she was needed to run the home. It was all her husband's fault. Ben Meany was still fond of his bed, generally only emerging from it to partake of his dinner. So long as he was planted there, her life was limited in its range of possibilities, social and educational reform not being amongst the most pressing of her concerns.

'Is the new powder helping with the pain?' she said to him that evening once they were alone.

'Ah sure, maybe it is. It was helping a couple of weeks ago when I started with it, but after you get used to these medicines and things in your body, the good goes out of them.'

'You must have tried them all by now.'

'Feckin feels like it. You think I wouldn't rather be out working like I used to? Sure it isn't easy for me either, Mary, stuck here like some…' imagination failed him '… like a thing that can't fecking move without hurting.'

'A limpet?'

'What?'

'Stuck like a limpet to a rock. Or a clam, perhaps. Or just glue.'

'What's the matter with ye? If I can't feckin move, I can't feckin move. The doctors don't know everything, you know?'

'I'll talk to the chemist when I get to Limerick. Maybe there is something that can help you.'

When Ben Meany made the mistake of waking up on the following morning, it was to a changed world. Mary had not brought his breakfast to him as she usually did. He made his way to their kitchen, in his usual, somewhat laborious, fashion.

'What's the matter with ye?

Mary Meany stood with her back to him, a letter in her hand. Time slowed for Ben as he recognised what it was.

'Is that one of mine, Pet?'

'I should think it is, *Pet*. I should very much think that it is one of yours.'

Her voice was cold and deliberate. Ben saw a collection of his letters sitting in a pile on their wooden table. For the first time in a very long time, he began to feel worried.

'These are mine, they're none of your business. What do you want with my letters? They're from the chemist in Limerick, about my medication is all.'

'The older ones are from your chemist, and your doctor, and the newer ones are from, unless I'm very much mistaken, a sweet shop. A! Fecking! Sweet! Shop!'

'Now if you'll only let me…'

'… Master Kenny says that reading broadens the mind, so let's do some reading and see if he's right.'

'Now then, you have no business looking through…'

'… "In my opinion there can be no justification for the continued administration of such strong medication for what is principally a psychological affliction. I must therefore decline your request for any further prescriptions." Six and a half years ago, this one was. Six and a half years, and you haven't been on anything, have you?! Have you, you useless, feckless arse of an excuse for a husband!'

'You know I'm not well. It isn't my fault if the doctors don't know what it is,' Ben offered.

'Is it not?'

'He says right there that I have a psycho, psychol…'

'Psychological affliction?'

'Yes, that. So there is something wrong with me, and it might be an injury to me brain. That's what he's saying.'

'That is *not* what he is saying. He is saying that there's nothing fecking wrong with you!'

'Now then, you don't read too good, and maybe you don't understand what it is.'

'Well.'

'Well what?'

'… Don't read too *well*. And of course I know what an affliction is, and you don't have any.'

'Well the doctor says I do.'

'And you've been treating it yourself, have ye? With fecking sugar powder!'

'It makes me feel better is all. I tried everything else, ye said it yourself.'

'To think I've been waiting on you, hand and fecking foot, all this time!'

Ben sat.

'I will not bring another meal to you, not this morning, and not ever. Get up now and go out and get a job, bring home your wages like any decent man.'

'I can't, Mary. I really can't.'

'You really *won't*, you mean. Well that is it, then. That's enough. I'm leaving you here, and you can rot in that bed of yours for all I care.'

Mary didn't know how furious she was until she heard her own words.

'I'm serious. I'm leaving. I've had enough of you. I'll go to Canada, I think, where I will have a good life with my girls instead of a miserable one with you!'

'You wouldn't do that to me, you wouldn't dare!'

'Stop me, will you? How will you follow me? You can't hardly move, remember. Look! A miracle! My husband has regained the ability to walk! Let me tell Father Henry about this new miracle in Bruff!'

'You've no idea what you're talking about, woman.'

'Have I not?'

'Who will look after the children?'

'Oh it's a bit late in the day for you to worry about that, don't you think? The other three will come with me.'

'We can't afford that!'

'*We* can't, but *I* can and *I* will.'

'God help me, I'll...'

'Another miracle! His strength is returned to him after all these years! Praise be!'

'Mary, you don't need to leave. I'll do better. I'm sorry.'

'Not nearly as sorry as you will be. You see, reading *does* broaden the mind. Good riddance to you.'

Mary Meany spat on the kitchen floor, and walked to the door.

Within days, a ship was carrying Mary and her daughters to Liverpool, from where they were taking the ship to Canada.

Ben Meany did not hear from his wife for a very long time. When he did, it was by way of a short letter to tell him that she had arrived and that the family were all well.

He never knew about the tears of joy when the family were reunited on the dockside. He never saw his children becoming adults. And he certainly never knew that his wife was teaching English classes.

Ben was left with little choice but to fend for himself. He did so with moderate success, eventually taking some pride in his work, such as it was. He never replied to his wife's letter, though, and he never went to Canada.

Chapter 16

There was only one big room for all the classes, which made things difficult for Trudy Fitzgerald, with children from just four or five years old sharing a room with those up to twelve and thirteen years. Behind the master's desk was a pot-belly stove, on which the pupils would put their glass bottle of tea to keep them warm on winter days. At one side of the room, there were desks made of wood with decorative iron legs, an ink-well at the top of the desk, which the teacher would fill with ink, and each desk would seat two children. There was one long stool at the top of the class facing the teacher, for oral work like prayers, poems, recitals, first holy communion classes and confirmation classes, and of course music.

The master was gifted at playing the fiddle and spoons; he also had an accordion, and a few tin whistles. The stool, or *furm*, was used to teach those instruments. Although the pupils did not posses any musical instruments, he would do his best. He would put on a musical evening coming up to Christmas, when the children would sing hymns and recite poems, and those who could play the tin whistle would do so. He played the fiddle, and one boy in the class had a beautiful voice and would sing. The entire room would fall silent as everyone listened. The same boy, whose name was

Lorcan Byrne, sang solo at Mass every Sunday morning with the organist, Mr Shortall.

Outside the school, there was a large yard with dry toilets at the bottom. It was up to the pupils to take care and keep it well swept. At the bottom end, there were two goalposts where the boys would play football.

When Father Henry came, he would sit at the master's desk and give a religious lesson. Each class would come to the stool and sit nervously, their eyes to the floor, afraid to answer any questions, and hoping that the priest would not pick them, as he would get angry with them if they did not know their catechism. Both the inspector and the priest's arrival was an upheaval in the school. The teacher would not tell his pupils until the day before they came, as they would otherwise have too much time to think about it, and possibly not turn up for school that day at all.

Mr Kenny put a lot of trust in Trudy. At times, she would lose control, and the children would start shouting and banging the desks. Trudy would stand on the master's desk and try to shout them down. At first, no one paid her any heed, but she told the master, and he soon put the pupils right about who was teaching them.

At home with her dad, Trudy would tell him everything that went on during the week. He was great to give advice, as he knew all the pupils' parents, and would recommend whom she should ignore, and whom she should help the most during the history and geography class.

Dick Fitzgerald looked forward to Trudy coming home at the weekends, and enjoyed hearing of the goings-on in the school. He was very proud that the master wanted Trudy to take over the teaching of some of the lessons. He could see that she was growing in confidence.

Dick also knew that she would go further than the local school. At the weekends, she began to ride out on the horses, and wanted to help with the grooming too. James was beginning to get slow. Trudy would ride off towards Dillons' wood, tie the horse to the tree and spend hours there all alone.

As time went by, the master gave Trudy more and more classes to teach. He wanted to have her trained up for when he would retire himself, or to stand in for him for those occasions when he felt unwell.

Mrs Kenny taught Trudy her table manners, and how to behave in a ladylike fashion. She also taught Trudy how to make a pattern for a dress and skirt. The material was all wool and very heavy, but such dresses were meant to last for many years, often being passed down from mother to daughter. Trudy was delighted with her new clothes. Mrs Kenny later showed her how to make many garments, and how to take measurements. Trudy was not slow in asking her father for money to buy fabric. She asked Mrs Kenny to purchase some calico to make a red underskirt, and enough material to make two dresses.

When they were not playing cards at night, Trudy and Mrs Kenny would both sit at the table and cut out the dresses. Trudy learned how to sew the pattern pieces together. At the end of the first week, Trudy had a beautiful dress in green with a red petticoat underneath. That Friday evening, she wore her new dress home. Her father was shocked to see Trudy in such fine clothes. He praised her work, and promised to give her more money on Monday morning. Trudy wore the dress all weekend, looking at herself in the glass each time she passed the mirror.

Between the master and his wife, Trudy was moving forward in the right direction. She became fond of Mr and Mrs Kenny. Monday morning was not to be dreaded. When she crossed the small bridge before the school, she would leave a stick on the stones, to let her friends know that she was in school already. If there was no stick, they knew that Trudy was not there yet.

Trudy now felt very comfortable in the Kenny home, and helped with the various chores as though she were their own daughter. The Kennys too looked on Trudy as their own child. The teacher and his wife did more than just teach the children in their school. If any child had a fall or a cut, they would be brought to Mrs Kenny, who invariably had a box with some soothing cream, and also some iodine and bandages. Often, the child who hurt him or herself loved going to Mrs Kenny because she treated them so kindly and would slip them a slice of cake. When the apples in the orchard ripened, she would fill a bowl and take it to the school at break time. The children thought that these apples were the biggest and sweetest they ever tasted.

Dick Fitzgerald would stop in once a week and pay for Trudy's keep. Since she had started to help out in the classroom, though, they had agreed on a lower sum. Trudy was fast becoming as indispensable to the Kennys as they were to her. Mrs Kenny was fond of buying her clothes, cutting her hair and ensuring that her boots and shoes were polished when needed.

Trudy continued to read everything the master would give her; her knowledge of history and geography growing and growing. He was in awe of her capacity to retain everything she read. He had a good feeling about this girl; she would go far in the world.

When she reached sixth class, the master asked her to now take over the job. She could stay on with them during the week, and he would be there to back her up whenever she needed help, either with the pupils or with some of the lessons. It was a good solution for Trudy. She did not want to stay on the farm and work like a man. She looked forward to going home at weekends, but that was it. If it were not for her ageing father, she probably would not go home at all.

She was known as Miss Fitzgerald the schoolmistress, and with that title came the admiration and respect of the community. She fulfilled the role just like Mr Kenny had done, parents of her pupils would coming for advice and form-filling, just like they had done before. She would discuss issues regarding pupils or parents with Mr Kenny and his wife.

Many years passed, and Dick Fitzgerald's health began to fail. Trudy could see him deteriorate gradually on her visits each weekend. He stayed in bed for hours, and sat smoking his pipe for longer than he used to. He was losing interest in the farm and the horses, and was just about keeping things together. When the summer holidays came, Trudy decided that she would help him to take an interest once again, which he did when she was around. Trudy grew from a young girl into an adult, and spent all of fourteen years in the partial care of the Kennys.

Trudy would make sure that her father had regular meals, would get him out of bed in the morning and take him with her when she went out riding.

Whenever she came close to Dillons' wood, Dick would turn around. He would not go within a donkey's bawl of that wood. Trudy tried to convince him to walk through the wood with her, but he got so nervous that she gave in.

On the ride home from Dillions' wood, Dick told Trudy the story about Michael Dillon and how he lost his eye when he went to cut back the bushes.

'He had just swung the scythe when the branch flew at him,' Dick said. He believed that there was some evil power at work in the wood.

'Well now, Daddy,' said Trudy, 'I have been there many times and I spent long hours there as a young girl. I never saw anything of any bad things going on. To me, it is a very safe place to wander through, and sit and look at the animals and birds.'

'Trudy,' responded Dick, 'you are some special person. It's only you who can go and stay there. The spirits are friendly with you. But I am still afraid for you, Trudy. I wish you didn't go there; you never know when the spirits might get angry and maybe even attack you. Even when I was a young lad, my parents would not allow me to go near that wood. I never did, in case I would disturb the spirits. I was afraid of what might happen, so I left it alone. I wish you would do that too.'

'Daddy, I am fine going into the wood,' Trudy assured him. 'I'm sure they would have done something to me by now. Anyhow, I'm not afraid.'

She discussed her father with James. James could see the deterioration in Dick, and explained to Trudy that Dick was aging and that this was natural.

One day, Dick called Trudy to the kitchen table.

'Close the door, Trudy. I don't want anyone coming in. I want to have a private talk with you.'

Trudy sat in her usual spot at the kitchen table. Dick loaded his pipe with tobacco from the jar he kept on the dresser, tamping it down with his thumb, and seeming to his daughter like an old man. Trudy sat quietly while her father went through what was to him a soothing routine. Once the pipe was lit to his satisfaction—and of late, he had few others—he was ready to talk with his daughter.

'Dad, tell me what's on your mind.'

He just sat for a few moments, allowing a narrow plume of smoke to escape from the side of his mouth.

'This is not easy,' he eventually said. 'It's time I tidied up my affairs. You are the only one I have left here, and I want to see that you get what I have. I want to make my will. We will have to go into Limerick next week and get things done properly. This land and farm has been in the Fitzgerald family for many generations. The way things are going now, the British are taking over the land and putting the owners off or making them take a one-way trip.'

Trudy was shocked to hear her father talk like this.

'It's too soon, Dad,' she said. 'You are not ready to give up the reins yet.'

'Well, Trudy,' he explained, 'I'm not getting any younger. I can feel my body closing down. I want to rest. Believe me, I am no hurry to go anywhere, but I will rest easier when I have this done, just in case anything happens to me. Otherwise, everything will go to the state, or maybe to your brothers, and they don't need a farm. But you may need the farm to sell; I don't want you to think you have to keep it. Because you don't, Trudy. Do whatever you will with it. As long as I can stay here and live out the rest of my life, that will do me. I have it all thought out, I know what I want done and will put it in the hands of the solicitor next week. I want to be buried with my first wife Catherine; I hope you will not be offended by this. I knew her for twenty-five years, and your mother Margaret for only a few years. I've thought about it, and it's what I want.'

Trudy's felt that the time was right to ask her father about something that had weighed on her mind.

'Dad, what exactly happened to my mother? Did she die after a fall down the stairs? I don't remember it.'

Dick Fitzgerald feared this question. He had counted himself lucky that Trudy had not asked him about it earlier. He suspected, quite rightly, that it was because she was not sure that she wanted to know the answer to it.

'Now is not the time to talk about this, Trudy.' Dick held his head in his hands.

'Look at me, Dad. I want to know how my mother died. I can hardly remember her at all. For years I've been trying to save her face in my mind, to make sure I don't forget about it. When I go to visit her grave, I find there is nothing there. Is she buried there at all?'

'Of course she is, Trudy. I have a Mass said for her every year on her anniversary.'

'I never knew about that,' she said.

'Well, Father Henry does it for me, and does not announce it from the altar. It's a private Mass, especially for your mother and no one else.'

'That Father Henry, I'm not too sure about him at all, Dad. He has an evil eye on him. He is a strange old priest. I bet he has lots of secrets. I'm sure he knows more than he lets on. He looks to me like he has one leg in the grave, although I'm sure he won't give up for a long time yet.'

'Secrets about what, Trudy?' Dick asked.

'Oh, everything,' she replied. 'From that confession box he must know everything about everyone.'

'I suppose he must.' He puffed at his pipe reflectively.

Trudy was not satisfied with her father's reply, and wanted to dig deeper. She suspected that there was more to her mother's death than Dick was telling her, and yet she did not want to push this frail man too hard. He had lost two wives, and had given his last ounces of strength to pay for her education.

'We will talk about this before we go into Limerick next week, Dad. What do you think? I want to know everything. I need to.'

Dick looked at Trudy.

'Some things are best left alone, Trudy. Let the dead rest in peace.'

He had never once thought of telling his daughter anything about her mother, but here it was again, back to haunt him. I cannot go through this all over again, he thought. It had been difficult enough back then. It began to dawn on him that he must put things right without devastating his daughter. Trudy really wanted to know everything about her mother, but if she did, then she would have to live with that truth for the rest of her life, as he had done. The child deserved better, and he knew it.

★★★

Trudy went out into the barn. She sat on a small pile of hay, her mind racing. She had not allowed herself to pursue the questions surrounding her mother's death for a very long time. My head has been in the clouds, she thought, I have been sleeping for all these years.

Thinking about how guarded Dick had been on the subject, she couldn't help wondering about what had happened. She looked around the barn. James was sitting up in the loft.

'You must remember my mother, James?'

James stepped away from the ledge.

'My mother. What happened to her, how did she die?'

'You would have to ask your father about that. I am only the workman here, as I was then.'

'Is there some secret being kept from me? It's my mother, James, I need to know what happened, and Dad doesn't like to talk about it.'

'Sorry, Miss, but I tell you I don't know.'

She would have to wait before broaching the subject with her father again, although she wanted answers. Her head told her that she would find out soon enough, but her heart was impatient all the same.

Trudy thought of Father Henry. That priest was no good. Could he have had a hand in this somehow? Something had happened, and now everybody was somehow covering it up. That much Trudy could tell. The priest had known her mother, and had been there somehow when she died, or so a fractured memory told her. She decided that she would pay that priest a visit.

In the meantime, Trudy had other concerns. She was not happy to learn of her father making his will. He was dwelling on leaving this world sooner than she would like. She concocted a plan to involve him more in her life.

Trudy asked Dick to help out in the school. She wanted teaching material for the children about the farmers and landowners of the area. Dick was excited about the project, and sat up by the fire for most of the night writing it out for her.

Trudy was delighted. Her father handed her the paper, smiling broadly.

'I hope this will be okay for your class.'

Looking at the paper, Trudy promised to use it that day.

'I'll give them till Friday to work on it. Well done, Dad. Next week I will ask you to write another, if you don't mind.'

Dick assured her he would be delighted.

That weekend, when Trudy returned home, she and her father sat and talked at the kitchen table, as had become their way. After catching up on each other's news, the question arose about the solicitor and the will.

'Do we have to do this now, Dad?' Trudy asked.

'Well, I would feel happier in myself if I had it all sorted. I will collect you at the school on Wednesday and we will head to Limerick. It won't take long.'

Trudy looked straight into her father's eyes and asked the question once more: 'What happened to my mother, Dad? Please tell me how she died.'

'Oh, Trudy, do you have to know everything?'

'Yes I do, Dad.'

Dick Fitzgerald had thought about what he would tell Trudy, and had decided that it was best to tell her what he and Father Henry had told everyone at the time. He did not want to change the story now, and perhaps hurt Trudy, but felt ashamed of what he was about to say.

With tears in his eyes, Dick looked into the fire and told Trudy that her mother had had a terrible accident in the house. A fire had started in one of the bedrooms, and her mother had run down the stairs to fetch water. She slipped and fell to the bottom, breaking her neck. He wasn't sure how the fire started. It was tragic, but there was little more that could be said or done. When he returned to the house for breakfast, he found her. Then Dick put his head in his hands and could not say any more.

Trudy was not sure whether she believed him. She did not press him further, but it still bothered her that he wanted to be buried with his first wife rather than with her mother.

Chapter 17

Numbers at the school were increasing steadily. Children came from many parts of Bruff to learn, including some older children who had never been to school and were illiterate. Trudy divided the classroom into two: one side for the newcomers and the other for the other pupils. She had the knack of making the lessons interesting, and made learning seem so easy for all the children.

Every evening, she would spend an hour or so planning out the curriculum for the next day, always leaving one hour for singing or playing any instruments they had. Every year there were first holy communion classes and confirmation classes. These made for testing times in the classroom, as Father Henry and Bishop Ahern would arrive to examine the children in their prayers and the holy bible.

The older children, aged between twelve and fourteen, had a lot of work to catch up with the children who attended young. Nevertheless, Trudy made a special effort to get them reading, give them homework and asked their parents to contribute to the learning, despite the fact that many of the parents were illiterate themselves. Some thought that education was a waste of time, that the boys would not need this to farm the land, and the girls would marry and keep house and have many children. Others were coming around to the idea that education was a good thing, as their children being able to read and write meant that they would be useful when filling out forms or making a lodgement at the bank. They would be able to read and sign documents, and not have to put an 'X' for a signature.

Trying to fit every child into the school and have a stool for them to sit on during class became overwhelming. Trudy decided to ask the master for help in dealing with so many children. She approached him that evening in his armchair while his was reading, his glasses hanging on the end of his nose.

'What book are you reading now, Sir?' asked Trudy.

'It's an old one, Trudy, *Great White Horse* is the title. Come and sit down beside me. How are things in the school? You seem to have many more pupils I see, how are you managing them?'

Trudy told him about the older children turning up for school, her difficulty in seating them all and getting books for them. The master took off his glasses and placed the book down on the table.

'My dear girl,' he exclaimed, 'what a great job you are doing with the children! Who would have known that the school would benefit from such a young person? It's your way with the pupils and the parents, not that the parents are too interested in what their children learn.'

Trudy blushed.

'Oh, Sir,' she said, 'it's not me at all; it's really you who showed me. You taught me everything. I am forever grateful to you. I love teaching; it gives me the chance to maybe change somebody's life. It makes me excited, you know?'

'Of course I do, Trudy. I understand. Leave it with me now,' said the master. 'I will think hard and hopefully come to some solution for you and the school.'

As the master began to fill his pipe, he thought about how fortunate the school had been to have Trudy there. Even the greatest of institutions, he reflected, so often come down to the willingness of a small group of people to do what is right; no more and no less than that. How Trudy found the energy to work so hard for the school and love each and every child there was a mystery. She even had the children learning how to play the tin whistle and the fiddle. While perhaps he was set in his ways, she would constantly try new things and new ideas, trying to change and improve things all the time, and more often than not succeeding. Trudy was a powerful young woman, no doubt about that.

'You're in a world all of your own in that chair.'

He had not heard his wife coming into the room.

'I'm only thinking is all.'

'Trudy?'

'What are we going to do with her? Poor girl. Her mother died when she was very young, I think she was only four or five. Her father is an old man now. Looking after him at the weekends and the children through the week is no way for one so young to spend their time.

'She has help at the farm.'

'Yes, I know him a bit. James, I think it is. That farm-hand seems to have been there forever, doesn't he?'

'Well it's a good job for Dick that he isn't alone. He isn't able to work like he used to. It's been working for them.'

She took a seat, feeling tired.

'James is there during the week, and Trudy is still there at the weekends. Dick has a lot of help.'

'We should try to help her, though. Hire another teacher perhaps. That would help her to deal with everything. I know what it's like. Schoolbooks, desks… there's no end to what you have to deal with. It's a lot for her.'

'She is remarkable, really, isn't she?'

'She certainly is.

At the dinner table, they discussed the various problems in the school. The master chatted away as normal about the school once again, this time offering solutions to the overcrowding. He would get a local carpenter to make a few stools and desks, he said, and would find out how much this would cost. He went on to suggest that some parents should contribute to the cost; some of the big farmers could well afford a desk and stool for their child, or children, as the case may be.

'That's a great idea, Mr Kenny,' Trudy replied. 'If we could get the parents to pay, just like they do in the church for a pew, that would solve the problem of the seating.'

'I will surely come up with some help for you,' said the master. 'If not, I will consult with Father Henry. He knows every person in the townland. The payment will be the problem. Father Henry is always on about the cost of running the school and how the parish struggles to keep it going. He never stops talking about raising money for this that or the other. But I'll give it my best shot, and try and convince him of the need for another teacher.'

Trudy did not want to share the school with a new person, although she knew that she could not handle all the pupils all the time. She wanted a say in getting another teacher. She asked Mr Kenny to let her know when they were interviewing for the teaching post. She wanted to sit in on the interviews if anyone turned up for the job.

Trudy left the table and went upstairs to her room. She sat on her bed. She breathed in deeply and exhaled slowly.

Chapter 18

School went well for Trudy. More new students turned up. Trudy had to put them off until she got new seats sorted. She asked them to come back next month; hopefully she would have a place for them then.

How many more children could be in Bruff, she wondered. Where were they all coming from? They were not at all from Bruff, she knew; some of them came from the next townland of Monart.

Things were getting out of hand in the school. Not every child had a seat when they all attended. Trudy asked the master for the stools that were in the parish hall to make do until she was able to get the money for new ones. The master brought what he could from the hall. The stools would have to be returned when they were needed in the hall again.

After a trying day, Trudy went into her room until dinner. She was feeling the pressure of her role in the school, and was struggling to manage it as well as making time to help her father. Trudy knew that he needed her help, but she also knew that she had responsibilities at the school now, and that her work there was important. After Mrs Kenny called her, Trudy entered the dining-room, where the master was already seated.

That evening, the master spoke to Trudy about the school overcrowding. He had been to visit Father Henry, and asked him for some extra stools and desks. Father Henry was slow to answer, explaining that there was little money to be had, that most of what he did have would be needed to get a new floor for the chancel, and that many of the children would not stay at school.

'It's just that at the moment, Miss Fitzgerald is teaching there. If she goes, which I think she will,' Father Henry had said, 'they will all fall away again and we will be back to low numbers. The people around these parts are not too interested in education; they would prefer their children to work and make their farms profitable.'

The master, however, had a different opinion. He reassured the priest that Trudy Fitzgerald would not be going anywhere soon. Her father was elderly, and Trudy was the only one to take care of him, and he was not in the best of health. Father Henry was not of the same mind.

'Let us wait and see. If she is here in a year's time, we will see if we can do more with the school.'

The master asked Trudy if she thought she would stay in Bruff teaching indefinitely, and was somewhat taken aback with her reply.

'Sir, I really don't know,' Trudy replied. 'If anything happened to my father, it would be different; maybe I don't want to stay alone on the farm. The landlords are taking over the farms and we might have to try and rent the farm back, or we could end up deported with a one-way ticket to somewhere far from here. If I go, I want to be able to choose where I go myself, and not have to go where I'm told.'

'You deserve better, Trudy. A lot of us do.'

'I want to have a voice and a choice in where to put down roots. I've been happy teaching in the school, but I don't know where I want to be in years to come.'

'But that is what you want, to put down roots?'

'Yes, I think so. I can't say that I have much of a plan, but I know that I want to accomplish something. Really try and achieve something rather than watching things go by.'

'You already have, Trudy. You should try and be happy with yourself.'

★★★

Trudy was finding her life at home with her father something of a struggle. At some point she had scarcely noticed, Dick Fitzgerald must have turned into an old man. He moved more slowly than he used to, drank a little more, and his house no longer looked, to Trudy, like the farm used to do. It was now largely abandoned, Dick only using those rooms that he needed and locking up the rest.

He was becoming more needy, and Trudy was afraid for his health. He had the worries of the owner of any kind of business, but had never been well equipped to deal with them at the best of times.

For his part, Dick relished the conversations with Trudy about the school and the Kennys. He found that his daughter was always able to surprise him with her dedication and her ingenuity, and his pride in her became his touchstone for thinking about his life. When he thought about himself, and such thoughts could quickly turn to the melancholy, he would think about Trudy instead, his Trudy, and everything she did, and everything she was.

Monday morning came around too fast, and Trudy was back at the school.

'English books out, please. Let's make a start with the spellings,' said Miss Fitzgerald.

At the end of the day, she gave a music lesson, with singing.

'We all need cheering up today,' she told the children. One forward boy stood and asked her was she feeling unwell.

'Not at all,' she replied. 'I am very well, thank you. Maybe just a little tired. It was a long weekend with work to do for my father. Sit down now and continue your music.'

The children looked around at each other, and some giggled. Trudy noticed, and asked what was the matter; of course none of the children would say what they were laughing at.

'All right then,' Trudy shouted, 'school is over for today. Get your bags, tidy up and bring your homework with you. I will see you all tomorrow.'

Chapter 19

That week, Dick called to the school for Trudy in the pony and trap. When Trudy came out, she was surprised to find her father dressed in his best clothes, freshly shaved and with his moustache trimmed.

'You look good today,' she told him.

'It's not too often I go in to Limerick, and it's once in a lifetime I will go to the solicitor and make my will! It's a big occasion for both of us.'

In Limerick, the solicitor's office had a distinctly musty smell. Books were strewn all over the place, nothing seemed organised. The solicitor sat behind a huge wooden desk, in front of a big, cobwebby window that stretched from the floor to the ceiling with shutters at both sides.

'Well now, Mr Fitzgerald, what can I do for you?'

The solicitor, Martin Brannigan, was a heavy man with a red face, boasting huge sideburns and a moustache turned up at the sides, along with ears that stuck out. His hair was combed over his bald head.

'I need to make my will,' said Dick.

'Well now,' Brannigan said once again, 'we will have to go back and check through the files and ledgers. Was everything done for you by your parents? Did they make a will before they died?'

'That I don't know,' Dick replied. 'I am the eldest son and inherited the farm from them. They're long dead now.'

'Do you have any papers to show that the deed was done?' asked Brannigan.

'No,' Dick replied. 'The farm has been in our family for generations. I want to leave it to my daughter Trudy here. I have some papers here, but they are old. I think they would belong to my great-grandfather, who was Richard Fitzgerald like myself.'

'I will have to go through the files and find your parents' will,' said Brannigan. 'This will take a month or so. If there is no will, as is often the case, we will have to administer for the land, and that could go back many generations, as some families have never made a will. Do you have other children? How many? Were you married more than once? What about sons, do you have any sons in the family?'

His questions came faster than Dick could respond to them. As the lawyer's pen flew furiously across the paper on his desk, Dick explained as best he could that his sons were long gone from home, and that his eldest was married into a big farm in the next townland.

'My other two sons have emigrated to Boston, and are definitely not interested in coming back to take over the farm.'

'Could there be others who may have a claim to the farm?' Dick shook his head. 'It will cost you a sum of money to get things in order, but we will start with searching the files.'

'The sooner, the better,' Dick said.

'We can't rush these things,' said Brannigan.

Trudy spoke up.

'No hurry,' she said to Brannigan, 'we will come back when you post us a letter.'

The solicitor asked Dick for a contribution of five pounds to start the search.

'That's a lot of money,' he replied.

Brannigan explained that it would take many hours to go through everything, and that his apprentice would do most of the searching, but that it would all add up.

Dick rummaged in his deep trouser pocket, pulled out some notes, got a five-pound note and handed it to Brannigan, who smiled.

'Nothing wrong with that bank you have in your pocket, Sir.'

'That is none of your business, Mr Brannigan. Do what you have to do and write to me when it's all ready.'

After the solicitor, Trudy and her father went to the grocery shop. Dick walked inside and asked for a pint of porter. Trudy waited outside the door, as women were not allowed in.

Dick took off his hat, and sat up on the high stool. Alongside him were four or five men drinking and smoking.

'Well, men,' he said, 'you all look happy here.'

'Sure we have nothing else to do only drown our sorrows. Our land has been taken over with British soldiers,' the nearest man told him.

'Where do you all come from?' Dick asked.

'The far side of Limerick,' one replied on behalf of them all. 'How about yourself?'

'Not too far. Bruff.'

Trudy put her head in the doorway. 'Dad,' she called, 'are you ready to go?' Dick swallowed down his pint. 'God be with you, men,' he said, and left.

While in town, they bought some washing soda, tea, polish for shoes, laces, flour and wholemeal for baking, as well as paraffin oil for the lamp. By the time they had everything loaded up, it was getting late and they set off home.

They were silent all the way home, hearing only the sound of the pony's hooves on the road. The journey home seemed to take longer than before; Trudy wanted to be home before dark.

James was standing in the yard with the rake handle under his arm, and took care of the pony and trap, helping to unload their provisions.

Trudy reflected on the day's events, as did Dick. James wondered at the humour of the two of them. He too was concerned about Dick, who was not his usual self, but James would not ask anything. He simply tended to the animals as instructed.

Trudy sat beside the fire, which was now little more than a few embers in the grate. She stirred them up and threw on some turf, her mind racing. She still had so many questions, and wanted answers. There were many old rooms, now disused, in the house, and she wondered whether she might find some answers.

She went to her bed, but tossed and turned for most of the night. Everything was going to change, her father was changing, and her life would not be the same for much longer. She needed to take stock of things.

The next morning at dawn, while Dick was still asleep, she began to investigate some of the disused parts of the old house, but found nothing in particular. In the parlour, she tried not to make any noise as she opened the door. Musty and dusty, the room was full of cobwebs. She sat on the arm-chair beside the fireplace and silently looked around. The light seemed different; the sun had come up and was shining in the huge window, illuminating the sideboard with the tarnished silver. Time had stood still in this room. Trudy had not been in the parlour for a long time. She wondered what her mother Margaret had done in this room. She came to the conclusion that her mother did little work in the parlour, and walked to the window overlooking a field that once was a lawn, now overgrown with weeds, briars and nettles.

The birds were singing, the cock began to crow. To the right of the window she could make out the barn, and beyond that were the horse stables. Beyond them was a path out of the yard and across to the wild moors; that too was overgrown with grass. Dillons' wood crossed her mind. She longed to go there, but that would have to wait. There was a big chest of drawers beside the window. Pulling hard, Trudy opened the stiff top drawer.

There was nothing much in it, just some embroidered linen tablecloths and crochet doilies. Everything was neatly stacked. On the bottom of the drawer was some sort of paper and the remains of mothballs.

The next drawer had cutlery, each piece engraved with the Fitzgerald crest. There must have been settings for at least twenty guests. It had been so different here once, but that world had all but gone.

The bottom drawer held a handmade bag that looked like linen, closed at the top with a piece of string. When she moved it a cloud of dust came up. She stepped back and coughed, holding her hand to her mouth so she would not to be heard. When the dust settled, she bent down on her hands and knees and pulled the bag out.

Trudy bent down to investigate more closely. She could see the outline of another drawer with two knobs; it seemed to be far back in the wall. Trudy stood up and tried to push the chest of drawers away from the wall, but it was much too heavy. She hunkered back down, and she pulled the knobs, but couldn't move them. The sun's light in the room began to move over the chest of drawers, and she could see a little more clearly. There was a tiny crack in the wood. She tried opening the crack with her fingers. It would not budge. Then she thought of the knives in the second drawer. With the knife, she managed to force the crack open. Stretching her hand and arm in as far as it would go, she felt something, and pulled on it. Out came a sturdy plait of hair, about a foot long and tied at the bottom and the top with a piece of string. The hair was brown at the bottom, going grey at the top.

She left it beside the linen bag, groped in again and found another plait. Trudy sat looking at this object, trying to decide what it was or if it had any significance. Thinking of the plaits of hair, she laid them down alongside each other. She really could not make out what they were doing there, or where they came from, but she did recall Mrs Meany talking about plaits of human hair.

Mrs Meany had explained that old women often cut off their hair when death was calling. She said that she remembered her own mother and her grandmother doing that. They put it safely into some hole in the wall of the home. It was said that when someone died and went on to the next world they needed their hair. There was some old folklore that said something about sinners coming back from the spirit world to collect their hair, and that it was very important to keep all the male hair-cuttings in a secret place so no else would find them.

Women never cut their hair, which would explain why the end of the plait was brown and the thick part was silver-grey. According to local folklore, hair was important, and should be kept safe for the spirit. It was well-preserved, but for how long she had no idea, and she thought that her father would have no idea either. These objects, like a lot else within her family, had been safely hidden out of sight for many, many years.

Chapter 20

Trudy was not able to sleep well that night. She thought back on the plaits of hair, buried in the old house. There was altogether too much that she did not know. Had her father told her the truth? Why wouldn't he? She struggled to think of a reason, but still sensed that he was holding something back.

When sleep eventually came to her, it was fitful, as she dreamed of her mother, trying to say something to her. She seemed to be far away in the distance, walking along a lonely forest walk. She looked lost.

Trudy woke in a fright, and sat up in her bed. It is a sign, she thought. Maybe mammy wants me to search for her, or perhaps she is not at rest. Trudy took out the prayer book and medals, and began to say the rosary for her mother, hoping that she would not be lost and lonely. Trudy felt that prayers would help.

The rosary was said, and the medals were examined once again, being used to bless herself. She sat back on the pillow, looking skyward for inspiration. She planned to search in earnest for clues to her mother's death. This house held too many secrets altogether, and she was determined to solve some of the riddles that had been on her mind for so long.

That evening, after their dinner, Trudy talked with her father.

'Daddy,' she said, 'I had a dream about mammy last night.' Dick turned quickly and looked Trudy in the eye.

'What was the dream?' he said.

'I dreamt of her walking in the forest. She looked lost and scared, like she didn't know what to do. It's hard to explain. I hope she is all right, wherever she is. '

'I will ask Father Henry to say a special Mass for her next Sunday.' He turned back towards the fireplace.

Trudy squeezed him on the shoulder. 'What happened to mammy? Did she really die from falling down the stairs? It's only twelve steps. Maybe you told me that because I was too young to understand, but I'm old enough now. I think about her, Dad.'

Dick's eyes were tightly closed, as if there were something that he didn't want to let in.

'I know that you are wise beyond your years, Trudy, but that doesn't change what happened. We all want reasons for things, but sometimes there aren't any reasons to be had. I wanted reasons too, Trudy, but I never got any either. I don't know how, but a fire started upstairs. Your mother was running down the stairs, I imagine to fetch water, and she fell and hit her head, and it killed her. The doctor said something about blood getting into her brain.'

'It's hard to understand, Dad. Why did it have to happen to you, to us?'

'Why indeed? That's a different question, child. If you ask how it happened, then I can tell you how. But if you ask why, I have no idea. Who does? Maybe there is no "why". There is only what happens. The "why" of things is a story we tell ourselves afterwards to try and understand. We want to fit what happens into a story with meaning, with a moral, with a reason. We want to shape things in a way that makes sense to us. But I don't know that there is any truth in any of it, really.'

Trudy stood, and did not reply to her father. She felt the emotions within her bubbling up to the surface, and threatening to break free. She turned to walk out of the door, and almost bumped into James, who was on his way in to talk to her father about something or other.

'It's a wet evening, Miss,' he said, patting Miller on the head.

'Is it? Yes,' she spluttered.

Trudy couldn't find the words to say, and half walked, half ran into the rain-swept evening, wishing that she could leave her troubles behind her.

As the rain continued even in the dwindling evening light, Trudy made her way towards the woods, the rainwater streaming down her face and mingling with her tears. In Trudy's world, things happened for reasons. When there were no reasons to be found, it wasn't because there were none; it was because she wasn't looking in the right places.

As she strode purposefully towards the woods, though she was not sure of her purpose, her clothes were soon wet through. She needed to calm herself, to dry out and to think. She made her way towards the old barn and stables.

As she walked inside, she was met with the malty smell of wet straw. Bales of hay and straw were stacked up against one wall, while the facing one was covered in James's farming tools. James's bedroom, or as near as he managed, was up in the hayloft above.

James was sure to be in the farmhouse for some time yet. He and her father didn't talk as often as they used to, but what talks they had would go on for some hours, dealing with the many affairs of running the farm. For a while, she would be undisturbed.

As Trudy climbed the ladder up to James's sleeping-area above, she became more and more conscious of her surroundings. She heard the rain lashing against the walls, and felt her wet clothes sticking to her, making her cold.

The few possessions James had were in piles on the rough, wooden shelves alongside his bed. Trudy made her way over to them, and began to rummage amongst them. What did she hope to find? She did not know. She only knew that so long as no answers were coming from her father, the only other chance was somewhere here. As she looked amongst the clothes and boots of a farmer, though, she started to wonder what she was doing there. Had she lost her mind, searching through James's belongings like this? What if he came back?

Trudy replaced the things as best she could, and started to make her way back to the ladder, when something caught her eye. One of the bricks near the bed looked different to the others. It was not cemented together in the same way as the others.

Trudy couldn't help herself. She went back up to the hayloft, and pulled at the loose brick. Sure enough, it came out in her hand. She looked nervously at the open door, blowing open and closed in the wind, but there was no sign of anybody.

Reaching her hand into the gap in the wall, Trudy could feel something. Instinctively, she knew what it was. She pulled out her hand, and was holding a large wad of banknotes. She could feel that there were others stuffed in the cavity in the wall. Could it be that they belonged to James? No, it didn't seem possible. He had worked on the farm for as long as Trudy could remember, but it seemed impossible that he could have saved up as much as this. Yet it made no sense that he would be working on the farm when he had all this wealth. What was keeping him here? Was he hiding from somebody? One thing was for sure: James had to know that the money was there. It was right next to his bed. Trudy resolved to confront her father about it immediately. Perhaps he knew what this was, or how James had acquired it.

Trudy replaced the banknotes into the cavity in the wall, carefully placing the brick back exactly as she had found it. Her heart and mind racing, she made her way back down the ladder.

As Trudy reached the floor, she heard the voice behind her.

'What do you think you are doing out here?'

She spun around, startled, to find James standing at the base of the wooden ladder. His hair and his clothes were wet, his trousers muddy at the knees.

'Nothing. I… I wanted to come in out of the rain.'

'Out of the rain.'

The light was beginning to fail outside as the rain continued to patter. As James spoke, his voice was calm, resolute. His breath could be seen in the cold air.

'And you thought you'd get out of the rain in my bedroom, did you?'

Trudy had never been so terrified in her life. James's tone was like nothing she had ever heard from him, or anybody else, before. He had that detached calmness of tone that only somebody truly furious can find, their anger bringing them to clarity of purpose. She looked around her desperately, but James stood between her and the only doorway.

'Look, I'm sorry, I didn't mean anything by it. I'm sorry…'.

James's dirty hand gripped her around the wrist so tightly that she couldn't move at all.

'What are you doing? Let go of me!'

'Didn't mean anything by it!'

'I'm sorry. I didn't see anything, really I didn't. And I won't say anything to anybody, I swear.'

'People like you never mean anything by it, do you?! I wonder what you might have been looking for up there.'

'Nothing, I wasn't looking for anything,' she sobbed. 'I just wanted to get out of the rain. I'm sorry…'

'I can't take the chance, little Trudy. It's a pity, really.'

Trudy lashed out at him, striking him in the face with all the force she had, and tried to run to the door. James, though, barely flinched, a cruel smile playing across his face.

'Bitch.'

'Let me go!'

She struggled against his grip, her clothes beginning to tear.

'I can't let you do that, little Trudy.'

Gripped now with panic, Trudy drove her knee up between his legs with all the force she had. He shouted in pain, falling to the floor, and she ran for the door, but James grabbed her by the ankle and did not release his grip, dragging her to the straw-covered ground with him. She tried desperately to struggle, but it was hopeless. James was twice her size, and his anger and rage turned to lust as he began to tear her wet clothes away from her body, his face now upon hers, one of his hands holding hers above her head helplessly as the other roughly made its way between her legs as she thrashed about, screaming for help.

'No!!!'

'You aren't leaving here, Trudy. Might as well get to know you better while you're still warm.'

'Stop it! Get off me!!'

She struggled, desperately writhing from side to side on the loose straw, pinned to the floor of the barn as he continued to feel her. He took his free hand away from her, slid his braces off his shoulders deliberately, savouring the moment, and then brought his hand back up to his face.

'You remind me of your mother.'

'No! Stop it!!'

Trudy clenched her eyes closed as tightly as she could. This was all happening somewhere else, she told herself, to somebody else, far away, but not to her, not now and not here. She imagined herself in the woods, and refused to recognise her body as her own.

'I've thought about this for years.'

'Think about this!' The voice belonged to Bob's Mary.

The last things that James ever saw were the two prongs of his own pitchfork, thrusting out into the air in front of him, driven through his back and out of his chest and throat.

Chapter 21

Bob's Mary had been on her way to visit James when she heard Trudy's shouts. Between the shouting in the barn and the lashing rain outside, nobody heard as she sneaked through the open door, as was often her way. Taking in the scene in an instant, she grabbed the nearest of the farming tools that hung from the wall, the pitchfork, and impaled James upon its prongs before he could complete his latest crime.

'Are you all right, Trudy?'

'Get him off me.'

Blood from the pitchfork prongs dripped onto Trudy's face as the two women rolled James onto his side, the handle of the pitchfork thudding against the ground, leaving James lying on his side, the spikes still sticking through him.

Trudy was breathless.

'I thought he was going to kill me.'

'I couldn't believe what I saw. Sure I knew he was a bit of a one, but nothing like this.'

Bruised and tearful, Trudy pulled on her clothes. They were covered now in dust and straw, some of them torn.

'Thank god you heard me, Mary. He was going to kill me,' Trudy repeated. Bob's Mary could see that she was badly shaken by what had happened. Even so, they were forced to confront the reality that lay just a few feet away, its dead eyes looking at the two of them.

'What are we going to do with him, Miss?'

'We can just tell the truth, can't we? He attacked me, and you saw it, and you came and hit him in self-defence.'

'Well now, miss Trudy. I've been to the courthouse once or twice, and they don't take too kindly to the likes of me, self-defence or no self-defence. We can't prove any of it. Maybe I just killed him and robbed him.'

'I don't know. I really don't know. Should we not just tell the truth? Why would I be lying about what happened?'

'Sure *you* might have no reason to be lying, but they would be pretty feckin' sure that *I* was. I've been there before, miss. The truth around here depends on who's feckin' tellin' it, believe you me.'

'Then maybe we make it look like an accident. We leave him over there, beneath the ledge. That way, he might have got drunk and fallen off it and onto the pitchfork. Or just rolled over once too often in his sleep, the bastard.'

'Help me with him then.'

Together, they snapped the handle of the pitchfork, as if it was snapped by his fall, and dragged James's body to beneath the ledge of the hayloft.

'We never speak of this again, miss. Whatever happens, we know nothing about it. It's just a tragic…'

'… Accident. Just an accident.'

And so it was agreed.

Trudy sat down on a bale of straw, her clothes torn and damp, her hair wet. She wrapped her arms around herself, trying to rub some warmth back into her body. It was a strange thing to think at such a time, but she found herself wondering how her father was going to manage without James. How were any of them going to manage?

Bob's Mary continued to rearrange the barn, dragging bales of straw towards its centre, and propping up some of the tools against them pointing upwards. When she had finished, she walked over to Trudy and sat down next to her, wrapping her arm around her shoulders.

'He deserved it, Miss. He never should have attacked you like that. Fecker can burn in hell for all I care.'

Trudy began to cry, and her tears were mixed with shivers.

'It's all right, love. He can't hurt you now.'

'He said something to me, Mary.'

'It doesn't matter what he said, lying pervert fecker.'

'Mary, he said that I reminded him of my mother. I mean, that...' she pulled her clothes around her, 'that... my body did.'

'Don't worry about what he said, Trudy. I'm sure he was just saying whatever he wanted. Men do, you know?'

'Why would he say such a thing?'

'Say what?'

'Why would he say that I reminded him of my mother like that? Did he attack her? Did he kill her because she said no?'

'How d'ye expect me to know such a thing?'

'You know a lot about *such things*. If you know what he was talking about, then for god's sake tell me, Mary, or I will be tormented by this for the rest of my life. You know something, don't you?'

Looking at Bob's Mary, Trudy could see that she was unsure of how to answer. She could see that she knew something, and was unsure whether to tell Trudy about it.

'Listen, Mary. The police will be here. I don't know what's going to happen, but I do know that they'll be here, and they will have questions about this. I need to know what you know about James, and what happened between him and my mother. Did he kill her?'

Bob's Mary breathed a heavy sigh.

'Your mother used to visit James here in this barn, Trudy. He didn't attack her; she wanted to visit him, you know. I'm sorry, Trudy. They were lovers. That's what he meant, about you reminding him of her.'

'How do you know, did he tell you? Did she?'

'They didn't need to. One night I was passing by, and I saw them together. Saw them at it, right where he lies now.'

'What would she want with him? She had my dad.' Trudy's mind returned to the hidden stash of money. 'Was he blackmailing her somehow?'

'I don't know, love. I don't think so. I *saw* them, and that's not how it looked. That's not how it looked at all, if ye get my meaning.'

'So did he kill her? Did my father find out, and he did it? I don't understand.'

'I can only tell you what I know, child. Your mammy got pregnant. It was obvious that she was pregnant. And I wondered about who the father was, you understand? Anyway, it wasn't long after that when she died. That's all I know about it, god's honest truth. Sorry business.'

'It couldn't have been my father, could it? He finds out about James, and then he confronts her and pushes her down the stairs. I can't believe that he'd do such a thing. But he hasn't told me the truth about it, Mary. Can I trust him?'

'Dick Fitzgerald wouldn't harm a fly, miss, and you know it.'

'I don't know what to think any more.'

'Your Daddy's a good man, Miss. I don't know if he knew about your mammy and James. Perhaps he did.'

Chapter 22

Sunlight was beginning to play across the front of the Fitzgerald farmhouse as Trudy returned from the barn. Dick, unable to sleep, was already awake, and Trudy smelled that he was boiling eggs for their breakfast.

'Where have you been? Are you all right? I looked everywhere for you.'

'Father… Dad… we need to talk.'

'Your clothes are torn. What has happened?' Dick was nervous for his daughter, and it showed in his eyes.

'I'm all right, Dad, really. But something has happened, and we need to talk about it now. Really talk. No more of these games, I can't stand it any more.'

'Come and sit down, Trudy. Of course I will talk with you.'

As the sun ascended into an uncaring sky, Trudy told Dick about what had happened with James. She told him how she had wanted answers about her mother, and how she had gone to investigate in the barn. She told him about the money she had found, and about how she was on her way back when James had arrived. As Dick struggled to contain his emotions, she told him about how James had attacked her, and how Bob's Mary, of all people, had arrived just in time to stop him.

'It's… unbelievable. Why would he do such a thing? Why now? After all I have done to help that man, this is how he…'

Dick stood up, clearly intending to pay James a visit.

'No, Dad. That won't be necessary. James is dead. Mary killed him. She stabbed him with his own pitchfork.'

Dick struggled to absorb this information.

'She did what?!'

'She had no choice! Anything less and he would have killed the pair of us.'

'Good god, Trudy. What have you done? What have we done?'

Despite her ordeal, Trudy seemed to be the one consoling her father.

'There's more.'

'More?'

'I know, Dad. I know about James and my mother. Mary told me. You knew about it too, didn't you?'

He nodded his head gravely, as if an inevitable defeat had been finally and mercifully dealt to him.

'I've been thinking about it all morning, and it all starts to make sense. You started to make sense. That's why you and James stopped being friendly. That's why my mother was treated so badly here, wasn't it?'

His eyes told her that she was speaking the truth.

'So what happened? Did you throw her out, or threaten her? I don't know everything that happened here, but I know that she didn't deserve to die.'

'You're right, Trudy, of course. I had hoped to spare you from the truth. I'm ashamed of myself, and ashamed of what I did. Your mother and me… we weren't happy together, not really. We didn't have much of a marriage; it was more of an arrangement. I think that I let her down. Anyway, I can't change any of that now. She was pregnant, and James was the father. Forgive me, but I didn't know what to do, Trudy. They were making me a laughing stock. I wouldn't have been able to leave my own house without people mocking me.'

'What did you do, Dad?'

Trudy's voice was trembling, her gaze intense. For a brief moment, Dick was reminded of their chess games all those years ago.

'I never harmed her, Trudy, but I wanted rid of her, I wanted her to get out. And she killed herself. Hanged herself in the bedroom upstairs.'

In all the time that Trudy had thought about her mother, this possibility had never occurred to her. At the least, it was no one that she had taken seriously.

'But you talked about a fire. I was too young at the time, but I still think I remember it. That was true, wasn't it?'

'Yes, child, there was a fire. I don't know how it started. Perhaps she started it, wanting to take me with her. I don't know. It might have been an accident.'

'How do I know you're telling me the truth now, Dad?'

Dick stretched out his hand, palm side up, in front of her.

'This scar is from the bed. I burned my hand on it as I was trying to help her.'

Tears began to run down his face. Tears that began their journey deep, deep inside.

'I tried to help her, but I couldn't, Trudy. She was already dead. And it was my fault. Mine and James's, perhaps. But I could have stopped it.'

'Why didn't you?'

'When I think about it now, I don't know. I was ashamed. I still am, even now. She deserved so much better than me. She was younger than me, Trudy, and was a lot of things. But I was never right for her. I should never have married her. But I am sorry for what I did.'

Trudy felt for him. Her anger with Dick and his dishonesty didn't change the fact that she was looking across the table at a vulnerable old man, full of love for her, and full of regrets. She wanted nothing more than to turn back the clock.

She fixed her father a drink to steady him, adding a piece of ginger and a slice of lemon into his strong whiskey.

'What is done is done, and we cannot change it now, Dad. What matters is what we do now.'

'Trudy, the police will be here, sooner or later. Will they believe that it was an accident?'

'I don't know. They can't prove anything though. How could they?'

'We should tell them the truth. Mary did it. They'll believe that easily enough.'

'We can't!'

'She's no stranger to the courtroom, Trudy. I'm only trying to protect you.'

'Mary is the one who did that. She saved my life, Dad. We have to help her.'

'Then we'll just have to hope they believe it was an accident. But they'll be coming for me, I know it.'

'For you? Why you?'

'Because I have a motive! This business between your mother and James. It gives me a motive, Trudy. Maybe I wanted revenge. Maybe I found out about it and decided to kill him. Maybe I should have.'

'Mary swore to me that she would say nothing about it, and I believe her. Why would she want to admit that she was there? She wouldn't, of course she wouldn't. They'd lock her up and throw away the key. There's only her, and us, who know about it. Except for us, nobody knows anything, do they? Do they, Father…?'

Chapter 23

Some things prove to be more easily shared with a stranger than with family, or friends, or even with one's husband or wife. Unburdening a heavy soul to a stranger comes with fewer problems, and without the concern that they might think less of you, or act differently towards you, in the future.

Two people in Bruff in particular fulfilled this role: one was of course Father Henry; the other was Bob's Mary. Few things happened but that they would be whispered into one of those four ears, sometimes more, and it mattered little whether it was in the intimacy of the confessional or a quiet field.

Bob's Mary was not surprised to be paid a visit by Dick and Trudy Fitzgerald, but was not entirely prepared for what they needed of her.

'Marnin.'

'Mary, I've told my father everything.'

'What would ye want to do that fer? He'll send me straight to the gaol, sure he will.'

'I won't. We need to talk, Mary. In private.'

Bob's Mary's house was not amongst the finest, but they were made to feel welcome there as she fussed around them.

'Sorry about the state of the place, Mr Fitzgerald. I just never seem to have time to…'

'We have a problem, Mary, and we need to take care of it.'

'I'll say ye've a problem all right. That's fer sure.'

'Father Henry knows, as I understand you do, about Margaret and James.'

Bob's Mary fumbled about, embarrassed to possess such intimate knowledge of the matter.

'I never told him nothing.'

'*I* did, Mary. It was foolish of me. I needed help at the time. I didn't know what to do, and he was there. I wish I hadn't involved the man, but I did. And now he knows. He knows that I had a reason to… well, he knows. And if the police don't come for you, they might come for me.'

'But sure Father Henry wouldn't want to tell them anything about something like that now would he? Sure there's nothing he wouldn't do for yer grand family and all.'

'I'm afraid that he might. We had something of a falling out after Margaret died. He wanted to send her to… He wanted to send here away for education, as he said it. And I went along with it. But after what happened, I blamed him for what he had done. He put us together in the first place, and then later he was sending her away. I blamed him for it all.'

'He had no business sending her anywhere,' said Trudy.

Bob's Mary nodded in agreement.

'But it wasn't just him. *I* went to *him* to ask for help. Maybe I shouldn't have, but I did. I involved that evil man in my family. What else was he going to do but send her away? I knew it before I talked to him. That's the truth. I knew what he was going to do.'

'You couldn't have known that he would want to send her away. How could you?' said Trudy.

'I did know. Or at least, I should have. I wasn't thinking too clearly. I panicked. It was easier to blame him than to blame myself.'

'Just because you asked him for help doesn't mean he gets to send your wife to be a slave in some feckin…'

'No, Mary. I asked *him* for help because I had already decided what I had to do. And it was wrong. I just didn't have the courage to see it through on my own. And later, I became so angry with him.'

'Well, sure what d'ye expect from a pig but a feckin' grunt?'

'We fell out, after Margaret's death, and now he would happily see me behind bars. Or you.'

'What do we do now?' said Trudy, who, despite her interest in the matter, was focused on the task at hand.

'Sure there's no telling that priest what to say or not say. He'll do as he pleases,' advised Bob's Mary, with an air of knowledge born of experience. 'He'll happily see us sinners in the gaol while they get hell ready fer us. And he all but runs that feckin courtroom, and I should know.'

With that, Bob's Mary nodded her head sagely in the knowledge of a point well made.

Dick looked at Trudy.

'Well, we have to stop him, one way or another. I won't let him do as he pleases with my family's life at stake. I will not.'

Trudy could not remember her father ever sounding so serious.

'Father, we can't cover up one crime by committing another one. And besides, there might be another way.'

★★★

The chapel was presently adorned with several pews, with the name of the Fitzgerald family proudly upon them, in addition to a most generous donation towards the fund for a new floor for the chancel.

Father Henry was of course curious as to how the struggling farm was suddenly able to contribute so generously towards the project, but not so curious as to be inclined to upset his benefactors with idle talk of the past.

Dick and Trudy had some concern that the priest might come back to them in search of more. What was to stop him? But as things turned out, they need not have worried. Just a few months later, before the new floor for the chancel was even completed, the body of Samuel Henry was found within the church. He had been strangled.

Rumours began to fly around as rumours do, but nobody was ever charged with the crime. The Fitzgeralds were fortunate enough to have an alibi, having chosen to stay in Limerick for a couple of days following their most recent visit to the lawyer.

Only Bob's Mary knew who had done it, and why, but it was one of the many secrets that she would take to her own grave.

Chapter 24

Trudy was not the same teacher as she once had been. The death of James on the Fitzgerald farm was of course the subject of much gossip and speculation, even before Father Henry followed him to an early grave. Many of the parents in the area began to whisper about Trudy Fitzgerald. Whispers turned into looks, looks turned into remarks, and a shared suspicion developed that Trudy was 'bad luck.'

For her part, Trudy had already been considering emigrating, and the decision now started to harden in her mind. She had considered America, Canada, Australia, but she kept coming back to the idea of South Africa. It would be a breath of fresh air to know that nobody, absolutely nobody, would know her, or anything about her. So long as she remained in Bruff, she would be unable to spread her wings and move forwards with her life. This meant talking to her father.

Trudy had talked with her father about her ideas of leaving in the past, but nothing was final. Now, however, she felt that it was time. If she didn't do it now, then she might never leave. And if she never left, then she felt sure that she would regret it later, maybe for the rest of her life. Trudy was afraid to leave, and knew that she would have to do so on her own, but she was more afraid of the regret she would be sure to feel if she stayed. Her father had lived with regrets for too long, and she had seen the effects of those regrets that she understood perhaps too late. She felt that she had to act.

'Are you unhappy, Trudy?' he asked, on being told of her plans.

'No, I'm not unhappy. I just feel that I need to do what feels right to me, and it feels right to leave.'

'You may be right. It hasn't been an easy time for you here.'

'I'm not looking for an easy time, just a new start. Nothing has been the same since… well, everything.'

'I understand, Trudy, I do. God knows you deserve better.'

'You could come with me, Dad. If you want to.'

'We both know that I'm not really up to it, Trudy. I wouldn't manage. It would be a long trip for an old man to take. And besides, everything and everybody I know is here.'

'Dad, I'm scared.'

'I know, love.'

'Will you manage here without me to help?'

'I'm sure I will. We have more money than we need now. I can hire somebody else. Somebody better.'

'You're sure you don't want to come with me?'

'Yes, I'm sure. I've always been here. I wouldn't belong anywhere else. I just wouldn't. You're too big of a person for this place.'

'Don't say that, Dad. I've been happy here too. I just feel that it's time for me to move on.'

'I know, Trudy. I don't want you worrying about me. It's not good for me to think that you are stuck here because you're worrying about me. I wouldn't want that.'

'It isn't like that.'

'Well, maybe not. But I don't want you to feel that you are stuck here on my account. I wouldn't forgive myself. You need to stretch your wings.'

Dick Fitzgerald got out of his chair and stood as tall as he could.

'Why would you not go and live with Michael, in Tipperary?' Trudy said.

'Never. I have my own place here and I will only leave it in the box.'

'Don't say such things.'

'I knew this day was coming, Trudy. Of course there's a part of me that doesn't want it to. We all want to keep our children with us. But there's more of me that is happy for you. And I really am. I couldn't be more proud of you, Trudy. I want you to be happy. You're the best thing that I've done with my life.

Trudy hugged her father.

Many a young man had stopped by the house looking for work. After James's death, everyone around the townland knew that Dick would need a young man to help him on the farm.

Eventually, he took on a middle-aged man who came to the door on one wet afternoon. Dick had not tended the horse that day. It was like it was meant to be.

The new workman came from the next village, and was married with a family. He had worked for a local farmer in his own area, but was forced to leave when the redcoats had come and taken over the farm.

Mick Brennan worked for Dick from Monday to Saturday. On Sundays he went home to his family. It worked well, as Mick could turn his hand to almost anything, often cooking the dinner for the two of them.

As Trudy walked around the old farmhouse, she felt the weight of its memories and hers at every turn. Its heavy mirrors, its wooden furniture. The objects surrounding her had been filled with such a lot of meaning, over the years. Eventually she found herself sitting on the floor, turning their old globe with one finger. Travelling the world was something that she had thought about all her life, and now she was going to do it, really do it. It was terrifying and exhilarating.

As Trudy looked around the house, she decided to take a few objects with her on her trip. She knew that, once she left, she would probably never see her father again.

Saying her farewells to the Kennys proved to be almost as hard as it was with her father. They were not surprised, of course. They had seen her grow into a fine and independent young woman, whose potential grew beyond the small school in bruff.

Mr Kenny returned to his teaching post despite his age, and it was several more years before he would find a suitable replacement for Trudy.

Trudy's pupils wrote a card to their teacher, wishing her well. It was hard to say goodbye. Trudy brought small gifts for every one of them, and promised that she would stay in touch.

For one last time, Trudy took a walk around Dillons' Wood. She had always felt fond of the place. It made her feel calm and at peace. As she sat beneath one of the oak trees, she looked at the card that her pupils had made for her. She could not stop herself from crying. They had written their names, and each had written a message for her themselves, in their own childlike handwriting. Every child there could write.

Slowly removing her hand from an oak tree, she turned and walked away.

Trudy had contacted the shipping company about her booking her passage on the next available ship. She had decided to go before the winter set in. She would be at home with her father for the summer months, but would not return to her teaching post at winter time.

South Africa would be her destination. It was a common enough voyage, with many Irish men leaving to fight in the Boer War. She found a big wooden trunk in the attic. Mick, her father's new workman, helped her to get it down, and she started filling it with her clothes. She sewed most of the money she had found, less their generous donation to the church of course, into the lining of two of her petticoats, hoping that it would be safe there. So long as she was wearing one of them, it seemed that the money should be safe. She had planned on leaving half with her father, but Dick insisted that she take it. In the end, she took the majority, but still left some behind for him, for her own peace of mind if nothing else.

When Dick saw the trunk on the middle of the floor in the parlour, his heart dropped.

'So the time has come,' he said.

'Yes, Dad. I want to go quietly, no gatherings.'

'I understand.'

Trudy had no intention of ever coming back to Ireland. On the last night at her home with her father, neither of them could sleep, so they kept each other company beside the fire, watching the embers glow in the darkness. Dick knew in his heart that he would never see her again. At daybreak, he decided that he would not escort her to Queenstown. He would stay and sit by the fire and pray for her safe trip. Trudy was happy about that; things were difficult enough.

At the kitchen door, she threw her arms around her father. She whispered in his ear that she loved him, and that he was not to worry about her because she was confident and excited about the journey ahead of her.

Dick managed to hold back the tears until Trudy left the house.

Chapter 26

Trudy arrived at Queenstown in good time. The dock was busy; many workers were loading the ship, and many passengers were waiting to board. She asked one of them to unload her trunk and get a porter to help her when the ship was ready for passengers. She held her purse close to her chest; now and again she would check her petticoat. She was happy to be on her way to South Africa at last.

She looked around, and walked up and down the dock. The day was bright, sunny and warm for late September. Trudy felt confident of her decision to leave Ireland and spend the rest of her life in South Africa. The unknown was a challenge that she embraced.

Forty-eight passengers in total were South Africa bound. There were twenty-one other passengers who were getting off at Liverpool. There were many families together, and some men alone, sitting on the boards and smoking cigarettes. Children were crying, couples bidding farewell to each other.

The foghorn was so loud and sudden that she nearly jumped. A shiver ran up and down her spine.

'All aboard,' the captain shouted. 'Women and children first.'

Trudy walked up the gangway, with her porter behind her carrying her trunk. This is it, she thought.

Once on board, Trudy was taken to her tiny and very basic cabin on the second deck named Emerald. When the trunk was settled on the floor, she hardly had room to move around. She fixed her tiny bunk-bed, and put her prayer book and medals under the pillow. She then knocked on both cabin doors on her left and right and introduced herself to her neighbours for the journey. Mrs Kearney and her husband John were a middle-aged couple, leaving home to find a fortune in South Africa. Cramped in the other cabin with little space for the three of them were Mick and Breda Flemming and their six-month-old baby Thomas.

These neighbours were concerned for Trudy travelling alone. Mrs Kearney was interested in everyone on the ship. She loved to gossip and find out where they came from and why they were travelling to South Africa. She took Trudy under her wing, advising her of the dangers of being alone in a strange world, and inviting her to come and make a start off with them in Cape Town. She wanted to employ Trudy to help her find a home and do the housework. Little did she know how Trudy had well-laid plans of her own in mind, and that nothing would stop her from following her own dream.

Later, Trudy climbed the stairs back up on deck. Her mind was moving forward to a new life.

The ship began to move away from the dock. There were people hanging out over the railings of the ship, waving goodbye to their family and friends, who were standing on the dock waving back and throwing kisses. Holding a notebook, Trudy began to sketch the dock from a distance. When she could no longer see it, she watched the land recede until Ireland was a shadow on the horizon.

The first night at sea was unpredictable, as the sea was very rough and unforgiving. One second the ship would sway to the right-hand side and the next it would sway to the left. Trudy got into her bunk and tried to sleep, but the swaying from the swell on the sea made her sick. At times, the ship was shaken so violently she could not stand up.

The first ship had sailed from Cobh, known then as Queenstown, in County Cork, reaching Liverpool two days later. From there, Trudy, known to her new acquaintances as 'Miss Fitzgerald,' boarded a ship bound for Africa. All going very well, the trip would take eight weeks, so long as the ship did not run into trouble off the Dover cliffs, as had been known to happen. Forty-eight passengers, most of them young families starting out on a new chapter in life, sailed from Liverpool that day.

The sea was choppy and rough, and even after the first ten minutes, many of the passengers had already started to feel sick. The captain went to visit them all in their cabins.

'I'm afraid that you will simply have to get used to it,' he told them. 'It's a long journey, and there's no other way. You will get your sea legs eventually and then you will feel much better.'

Despite the captain's words of encouragement, though, most of the passengers were seasick for days or even weeks. The captain ordered a bottle of brandy for each cabin, and told them not to eat anything for at least three days, until things settled down. Some people felt better more quickly than others. Miss Fitzgerald recovered rapidly, and left her cabin to take the air on deck. She was a strong woman, and refused to be fazed. The sickness was bad, but on reading and preparing for her trip she had acquired some knowledge of what was likely to happen, so at least she was mentally prepared for it. She refused to show any weakness, even to people whom she would probably never see again. As a woman on her own, she had to be tough and be seen to be tough and not let seasickness stand in her way. How could she prosper in a foreign land, if she were not even prepared to put up with a little discomfort on a ship?

So Miss Fitzgerald braved it out, and was among the first to recover and find her sea legs. From early in the journey, she was to be found on the deck gazing out to sea—always towards her destination, never back towards Ireland. When they began to draw near to the land, she asked the captain or his first mate about the things she saw. In her diary, she recorded her impressions of the journey and kept a log in her notebook of each day's happenings and the progress that the ship had made. She also tried to draw a map of all the landmarks they had passed, and she had a hand-drawn map of her entry into Port Natal.

Trudy Fitzgerald arrived at Port Elizabeth after an eight-week voyage. She was exhausted, and disembarkment seemed to take forever. She waited on the deck with all the other passengers. After anchoring the ship, the swell on the sea made it necessary for the passengers to disembark into a small boat alongside, and then to the makeshift dock, women and children first.

The captain stood on the gangway and wished every passenger good luck and good fortune. He had noticed that Trudy was travelling alone. He pulled her aside.

'I see you are on your own.'

'Yes, I am,' she replied.

'Port Elizabeth is no place for a woman on her own. There are many dangers out there. You will be a target for robbers and scoundrels alike.'

Trudy assured the captain that she knew about the dangers and was prepared to protect herself.

Once off the ship, Trudy looked around at the men who were looking for work, or just to carry her trunk. There were many, mingled together with the smell of the dock and the seagulls swooping down to pick up whatever food they could get. She was wearing her long tweed heavy skirt that she had worn all the way from Ireland, but it was just too hot. Her clothes would need to be changed to accommodate this new climate, but there was little she could do about that for now.

Trudy sat down on her trunk, and observed the locals. She picked out three men to help her find a place to stay. Her plan was to build a hotel with the money she had found, and now she needed to find the best place to locate it. There was no time to be lost.

Trudy's first night in South Africa was spent out in the open. The sky was clear with a full moon. She set up camp overlooking Port Elizabeth, with her workmen bedded down for the night. Trudy lay on the ground, but did not close her eyes all night.

Early the next morning, she had the men up and ready to move forward. She had bought a map from the captain's mate, which was little more than a rough sketch of the area. Trudy and her men headed south, without any food. They came to a small town where Trudy bought some food, bread and some dried beef. She and the men had breakfast together.

She noticed the men watching her when they thought she was not looking. They were used to taking a young woman to a hotel or boarding-house from the ship, but never like this, walking for miles in the hot sun. They were actually a little scared of Trudy. They had never seen long red hair and green eyes, so they jumped whenever Trudy asked for anything. They wondered whether she had strange powers—a woman travelling alone around Africa was unheard of.

After three days' searching for the perfect place to build her hotel, Trudy decided to return to the spot where she had stayed on her the first night on African soil. The men thought that she was taking them back to the ship.

Standing on the highest spot overlooking Port Elizabeth, Trudy decided this spot was the best place to begin. It was waste ground. She thought no one owned this bit of land, which was about five acres.

There was a lot of work, and great excitement around the town. The workers had just finished the first two miles of railroad out to the Kimberley mines. They were enjoying a break before they started on the next two miles of railroad.

Trudy walked to the centre of the town, looking for the municipal council. It was a large building, with many windows to the front and a huge front door with glass above it. Inside, there was a plaque on the wall telling her which offices were where. The planning office was on the top floor.

She climbed the stairs, entered the office and stood at the counter waiting for someone to attend to her. She noticed that the people working there were all men.

A Mr Brennan came to her assistance. Trudy told him of her plans to build on this plot of land. She wanted to purchase it and get planning permission for a twenty-bedroom hotel.

Mr Brennan seemed shocked, repeating Trudy's request slowly.

'That is what I want to do,' she said patiently.

'But no woman comes into this office looking for anything like this,' he replied incredulously.

'There is always a first,' said Trudy.

'Well, it's going to take time to look into this for you,' he replied. 'You would be talking about a year or two to get this straightened out.'

Trudy explained she did not have time to wait that long; she had no home and was in a hurry to build and get a roof over her head.

'Unless you break the law, there is nothing we can do for you,' Mr Brennan told her.

Trudy walked out of the office with a feeling of frustration. Could she simply begin building, trusting that she would be able to make it all legal later on? No, somebody else would then claim to own the land, just as had happened back in Ireland. After some thought, she decided to try a different approach.

She returned to the office on the next day, asking for Mr Brennan again.

'You again?' He was surprised.

'I wondered if some money might help me with the planning permission,' she told him. 'Maybe I can give you one hundred pounds, to help your family.'

The man was surprised, but not so shocked that he could not ask Trudy for two hundred. In return for this, he would see to it that they would turn a blind eye to the building. She gave him the cash.

Had she been foolish to trust a stranger once again? Trudy thought not. If Mr Brennan could be bought for two hundred pounds, then other types of men could be bought too, who would happily make his life unpleasant for a lot less.

On her way out of town, Trudy stopped at a building surveyor's office with the name Rory Armstrong on the plaque by the door. She employed them to draw up the plans and start building. Trudy then got a room at a boarding-house, where she spent the next two years while her hotel was under construction.

The men sitting around were shocked when Trudy asked them if they were looking for work.

'I am building a hotel,' she explained, 'and need skilled craftsmen.'

The men merely looked at each other, jumped up and followed.

Trudy had her own ideas about the layout of the rooms, and what materials were to be used, to which the builders from Rory Armstrong would not always agree. Trudy had to stand her ground and remind them that this was her building and they were to do what she wanted.

About one month into the build, Mr Brennan called to the site looking for Trudy. He wanted more money.

'Get out of here!' Trudy shouted at him. 'You have got all you are going to get from me!'

'I underestimated the cost of turning a blind eye,' he told her.

'Very well,' Trudy replied. 'Although, perhaps I should pay a visit to the town hall to let the other men know how much you have received already?'

'I really need the money,' he pleaded. 'I can stop everything here if you don't give me what I want.' He watched her carefully. Trudy would not back down.

'I told you to get out of here. There is no more money for you. And that is that.'

Brennan walked off the site, his head down. Trudy's foreman came over to her to ask if she was all right. Trudy looked at him squarely.

'There is nothing or no one going to stop me building here. He can come and go as he pleases, I will never give in to him.'

That was only the first of many run-ins Trudy had with the powers that be from the town hall. She remained determined to continue.

Chapter 27

As Trudy's hotel and prestige grew, many wealthy men came along seeking to invest with Trudy, but she would fend them off. They did not take kindly to her refusals, and tried and tried again.

Once the foundations were in, the building looked huge. There were some delays during the build. The slates she had ordered from China spent weeks on the high seas, while the building could not go ahead until the roof was on. Trudy intended to build on more bedrooms when she had made some money. Already she was being asked when it would be finished. Companies wanted to hire her hotel for functions and meetings.

Men coming in from the mines could not wait for it to finish. The hotel was a site of considerable interest in Natal. Rich men would come just to watch Trudy giving orders to the workers. They wanted to hire her to build them a splendid house. She got many, many offers and turned all of them down. One among them was Billy Monroe. He was one of many who were beginning to see Trudy as a powerful, bright and smart woman living among them.

The windows and doors were made by local carpenters. At one point, Trudy had a small army of over a hundred men working for her. The front doors to the hotel were about seven feet tall with celtic carvings on the centre and on two wooden pillars that stood tall at each side. Inside, there was a grand foyer with a reception on the right. All the materials and colours were red and gold and black. The local women made the curtains, which were very heavy velvet with striking tiebacks on each curtain. A huge, magnificent stairway began in the centre of the foyer and curled skywards to the top floor. The stairs also had many carvings of ancient symbols, some celtic like the front entrance. Other carvings were of local interest, ships and people. Each carving was expertly done with some gold leaf to enhance them.

Trudy chose the best materials available. Marble was her first choice for the floors. The stone was cool underfoot, and easy to keep clean. For the furniture, she went down to the docks and asked many ship captains to bring her furnishings from India and Italy and some other countries. All her soft furnishings came from Turkey. It was an international hotel furnished with items from different countries.

Ship captains were interested in staying at the hotel. They hoped she would finish building and open up soon.

Naturally, Trudy attracted romantic attention from men. She ignored them all. Billy Monroe, who was in the building trade, was one who really took a shine to Trudy. He would turn up at the site and give Trudy good advice. Trudy liked Billy, but Billy had other ideas. He told Trudy that he was falling in love with her, that he had never met anyone like her; he wanted to be by her side for the rest of his life. On hearing this, Trudy told him to leave and not come back again. He was persistent and kept returning. Eventually, Trudy had him removed from the site and banned him from ever coming back. Whenever the workers saw him coming they would put him out, and he finally understood and left Trudy alone.

In the garden at the back of the hotel, Trudy had seating carved from stone. This had never been seen before in any part of Africa. The stonemasons also adorned the seats with flower carvings that took considerable time and expertise. A fountain in the centre of the garden spouted water up into the air, which fell down as spray. This was very popular with both men and women on the very hot days during the African summers. They could walk in under the spray to cool off.

Trudy worked night and day to finish her project. Two years and three months after her arrival on African soil, Trudy opened her hotel. She hosted a party on the first night, and invited the most influential people in Port Elizabeth. This was her business strategy, to put her hotel on show.

Everyone was waiting for this moment. The people were stunned by the opulence and grandeur of the building, the beautiful garden and grounds.

Trudy had gallons of champagne, along with the best brandy and whisky she could find. The food was all local, with beef, chicken and many fish dishes. Trudy made sure she spoke to everyone that night. Some people were shy of her, but she soon overcame that. She made everyone feel welcome. This set the scene for her future clientele.

Only local men and women were employed. Trudy had eighty employees, who looked after every part of the hotel: footmen, parlour-maids, chambermaids, reception, butlers, kitchen and laundry staff.

All of the hotel bed linen came from India. Trudy felt the quality was superior to anything she has seen. She remembered how sheets were made back in Ireland, with the flour bags sewn together and then boiled for hours in washing soda to try and get out the product name.

The hotel laundry was huge, at the rear of the building. There were big tubs with steaming boiling hot water and a big wooden handle to keep the clothes turning around.

Sheets and pillowcases were put through rubber wringers, then hung on railings attached to the ceiling the length and breadth of the laundry room. Washing and ironing went on all day, and sometimes into the night.

Every member of staff worked away with no instructions. Trudy trusted them to do the best job. All of the staff were happy, and loved working for Trudy and the Royal Hotel.

After going strong for five years, Trudy decided it was time to expand. She left some land to build on when the time came, and planned another eighty rooms—such was the demand for her hotel. This new building was to the right of the main building. This time, Trudy employed a builder to take care of all the building and did not step in herself until it was time to finally purchase the furniture and decoration. She used the same theme in the new building. Now her staff grew to over one hundred.

Many of her staff married each other. Trudy allowed them to stay at their jobs and become part of a bigger family. She loved each and every baby born under her roof, and there were many. She made a special party for the christening of the babies. Some were called after her, of which she was very proud.

When the fourth Trudy came, she spoke to the parents.

'We have too many Gertrudes. They will be confused with one another,' she told them. On being asked for her suggested alternatives, she proposed Kathleen, Margaret, Bernadette or Theresa. These soon became popular names in the area. Boys were William, Richard, John, Martin or Stephen. All good Irish names for hard-working Africans.

Trudy had the first motorcar in the district. She employed a chauffeur, and took great pride in going for a drive in the afternoons around Natal. People would stop and stare as she went by, their mouths open in amazement. Trudy Fitzgerald was now becoming the wealthiest woman in South Africa. She was still getting offers of investment and to buy her hotel.

Some of her guests had struck gold, and were wealthy in their own right. Trudy made the miners very welcome, and had everything laid on for them. She spared nothing, the finest food and the finest wines and whisky, brandy too. Cuban cigars were a speciality.

Every guest dressed for dinner, during which they were lavished with the most delicious dishes, all served on silver platters. The maids served the food while the men served the wine and drinks.

The waiting staff wore a black and white uniform. The men wore black trousers and white shirts with black ties, and a white towel over their left arm. The women wore long, black dresses with a white collar and cuffs. Their hair was tied up in a bun under a white cap.

When dinner was almost over, Trudy would enter the dining-room, often to applause. Hotel guests would frequently compliment her on the fine wines and the glorious food. She would call her butler and ask him to hand out the cigars, and a second butler would follow to light them. The room would fill with laughter, and sometimes someone would sing. There was a piano and a pianist, ready to play when asked to do so.

Trudy would not have the musicians intrude; it was up to the guests to ask if they wanted some music. She would stay long enough to meet everyone present, and guests would have the opportunity to meet the legendary Trudy Fitzgerald.

★★★

On one particular Tuesday morning, ten years or more since she sailed to South Africa, the post was delivered as usual. There was a letter from Ireland. Trudy sat down on her office chair and opened it slowly. The letterhead read Brannigan Solicitors, Limerick City. She only had to see the familiar letterhead to know exactly what it meant.

Her father had died over a year previously.

Trudy held the letter, tears welling up inside. She put the letter down on her desk, sat back into the chair and cried for a long time. She had known that this news would come, but had thought that she would somehow be more prepared, but she was not. Trudy felt alone and disconnected from Ireland and her father.

Her maid came to bring her some tea and biscuits, as was their usual practice. Trudy pulled herself together as best she could and drank her tea. She read the letter. Brannigan had outlined the death and the cost of her father's funeral. She hurried to the cupboard behind her, searching for the last letter she had received from her father.

She had them all together in a tin box. She hadn't realised that it was almost two years since she had heard from him. At that time he was not well, but then he always complained of not being well. He was in his nineties. Mick had still been looking after him, and Ben Meany, of all people, would call every week to help him do the washing. Taking the letter in hand again, she read on. The will was there too, the one that she and her father had made all those years ago. On the next page, it told her of where the farm and house had been taken over and landlords were renting it out. This happened after Dick's death; Trudy was relieved that he had not been forced to experience that. At least he got to stay in his own home, she thought.

There was nothing left, Brannigan said, only he wanted payment for his work in looking after their estate for many years. He sent his condolences, saying that her father had enjoyed a long life and that he was buried with his beloved

Catherine, as was his wish. There was no mention of Trudy's own mother, Margaret. Perhaps he felt that she would not rest in peace with him there next to her.

Trudy searched for the prayer book and holy medals she had brought with her from Ireland. She laid them out on her bed just like she had done as a child, then knelt down at the side of the bed, said her prayers, then blessed herself with each one of the holy items. She prayed for her mother and father, that God would be good to them.

Did my father prefer his first wife to my mother, she wondered.

That evening, Trudy had her driver take her to the Catholic priest, Father Nolan. She asked for a private talk with him. The priest was very happy to meet Trudy, as he knew of her wealth and her hotel. Trudy asked for a Mass to be said for the repose of her parents' souls.

After ten minutes, Trudy handed the priest an envelope containing money.

'Take that for your church,' she said. 'Remember my parents often. It's what they would have wanted.'

She walked into the chapel and lit several candles, then knelt at the altar in fervent prayer.

The news of her father's death was a shocking blow. It would take her some time to get over that.

Chapter 28

'What about your uncles and aunts? Are they rich like your father?'

'On my mother's side I have two uncles, Gerard and Joshua, and an aunt, Mary. On my father's side of the family, I have one uncle, Noel. He never married and is in a home now for the elderly. I visit him once a month and take my father too. They are twins, they look exactly alike. Years ago I heard them talk of another brother they had, Martin, but I don't know what happened to him.'

Trudy was sure that this was her grand-nephew. How on earth did he come to this country, let alone her hotel?

She went to retire for the night, bid the young man goodnight, but turned back to him.

'Will you be here for a week or so?' she inquired.

'I will stay at this hotel for ten days. Then hopefully I will move towards the mines.'

'Would you have breakfast with me tomorrow?' she asked. 'Eight o'clock?'

The young man lit a cigarette, and slowly released the smoke. Many thoughts ran through his mind.

'Yes, let's. I'll see you then.'

He walked back to the bar where some men were having a nightcap.

'Sure you must've struck gold,' one of them said. 'Miss Fitzgerald doesn't talk with just anybody.'

Richard smiled. Throwing back his brandy, the man continued.

'That woman is the wealthiest woman in South Africa. She is the greatest businesswoman I know. She couldn't put a penny wrong. She built and owns this hotel.'

Richard had the reception call him at seven the following morning. He tossed and turned for most of the night, unable to wait for morning to come.

Trudy had no sleep at all. She got out one of her bags that she had brought from Ireland, searching for letters and documents she had kept. As she read through them, Trudy cried and laughed at the memories they evoked.

She had been thinking only recently about what she would do with her great fortune. Now, perhaps, she had found a Fitzgerald who might be interested in running the business after her, and carrying on the Fitzgerald name.

★★★

Long before eight o'clock, Miss Fitzgerald was sitting waiting for the young man to appear. She sat in a position in the dining-room where she had a good view of all the guests. She watched Richard enter. She had told the waiter to seat the man from room 106 at her table. Richard was so like her father Dick Fitzgerald it was uncanny.

With the broadest smile, he walked tall towards the table.

'Good morning Ma'am. I hope you had a good night's sleep?'

'Sit down,' she replied. 'How about you?' she asked.

'Oh yes I did, I can't get enough sleep these days. It must be the South African sea air.' This was not the truth, but he did not want to suggest that there was anything uncomfortable about The Royal Hotel.

'I would like to spend the day with you,' she said. 'If you have no pressing engagements?'

'No, not at all.' Richard was surprised. 'I would love to spend the day in the company of a beautiful lady, thank you.'

'After breakfast we will go to my private rooms, I have some papers to attend to.'

'You are a busy and powerful woman,' said Richard.

'I came from humble beginnings,' she said.

Richard could not see any traces of humble beginnings on this woman's face. She appeared to have it all, with her wealth and her fabulous hotel.

After breakfast, they both went to Miss Fitzgerald's rooms. On the first floor she took her key out, and opened the double doors into her parlour. Richard entered into the most beautiful room he had ever seen. Plush red velvet curtains hung from the ceiling to the floor, and there were two large couches in red and gold velvet. A beautiful mahogany table stood in the middle of the room, with decoratively carved and upholstered chairs. If anything in this room seemed out of place, it was the antique globe standing on a table in the corner.

Richard was stunned.

'I have never seen such opulence in any house. I guess you are a fine wealthy woman, Miss Fitzgerald.'

'Never you mind about my wealth, that's not important right now. Make yourself comfortable on the settee over there.'

She sat down behind her desk to sign papers and open the post.

'Has any of your family gone back to Ireland?' she asked.

'No,' he replied, 'not that I know of. Have you gone back yourself, Miss?'

'No, never. I never will. My home is here in South Africa. When I came here, I promised myself I would never leave.' She smiled. 'Anyway, who would run the hotel and keep the staff busy? This place would fall apart if left for more than a week. I have good and faithful staff, but they need direction. I began this hotel with faithful staff, they have made it and cared for it like it was their home too. I look at them as my own family. They also take me for their family. I employed the parents and now employ their children, and they are very loyal workers. They have married and had children here without ever leaving.

'When I first began to build, I was lucky to find good workers, carpenters, stonemasons, wood turners, painters—every trade I wanted. I had many advisors coming to the site almost every day. Local business then took a great interest in what I was doing. Some of them may have thought a woman could not do this work. I was the talk of the town, the "crazy lady building the hotel". I spared nothing on the building, and made the best choices on everything for the hotel. It has been quite a job.

'At first, I built sixty rooms with a laundry, a bakery and kitchens with huge cookers for the chefs. After five years, I decided to add another sixty rooms onto the hotel. My business was growing fast, and I couldn't keep up with the demand for rooms and functions and meetings. I had some delays on both builds, especially with the carpets and the furniture, which I purchased from other countries and had shipped here. The Royal Hotel meant everything to me, and still does today.'

Richard was beginning to wonder what was coming.

'I have something else to tell you' she said.

'I hope it's all good,' he replied nervously.

She paused, then took a slow, deep breath. Looking down at the floor, she said, 'I am almost one hundred per cent sure that you are my grand-nephew.'

Richard was shocked. He opened his mouth to say something, but nothing came out. He swallowed and tried again, looking straight into Trudy's eyes.

'How can that be? I have never heard of you in my family gatherings back home in Boston. My dad, he doesn't know about you either. If he did, he would have mentioned you.'

'No, they don't know about me,' she replied.

Richard put his elbow on his knee, resting his palm on his cheek.

'Jesus. That's unbelievable. Where did you come from? Sorry. I meant to say, where in the family did you fit in?'

'I was born after your father left Ireland and emigrated to America, my father Dick Fitzgerald told me that I had two uncles, twin brothers who had left Ireland to find work in America. He was always very sad when he spoke about them. They had to go because of the famine, and there was no work to be got around Bruff. A lot of young men and women left Ireland at that time, and most of them settled in America, Canada and Australia.

'When my father's first wife Catherine died, my father married again and then they had me. I am an only child. My mother died when I was very young, so I had to grow up quickly. I don't know why my father never told you about me, or my mother. He got letters from the boys, they always sent him money. Dick would open the letters and paper money would fall out. He would sit and read the letters in his chair by the fire, over and over again. He wrote back, and I would go to the post office and post it for him.'

All day long, Trudy and Richard talked, Richard trying to remember things about his grandfather. He knew that he wrote letters home to Ireland, but had never questioned him about them.

Richard's head was in a spin with all of this new knowledge. Then he remembered something.

'Now I think about it, Great-Aunt,' he said with a smile, 'something just came to my mind. I remember my parents talking about Eddie Malone and his wife Lola. Their daughter Sofia is my mother. I think the Fitzgerald men and the Malone man were always close friends, and met up often in our house. That's where my father must have met my mother I think.'

Later in the evening, she asked Richard to take a drive with her in her automobile. They sat side-by-side in the back seat of the car while her driver John drove them around all the scenic spots of Port Elizabeth.

Richard was very impressed with his aunt Trudy. For the next several days, they spent every hour together. Richard was so intrigued with this aunt, about whom nobody in the family had ever told him anything. For herself, Trudy very much enjoyed reminiscing about the past, and then she would bring up the future too. She found it almost incomprehensible that Steady Eddie Malone was this man's grandfather. It was as if the two worlds that Trudy had kept so separate in her mind insisted on being knitted back together as part of the same globe after all.

Finally, one morning while having breakfast together, Trudy asked the question that had been in her mind since the evening she met her grand-nephew.

'I am getting on in years,' she said to Richard. 'What would you think of working as my manager for the next few years and getting to know the business? With a view to taking over the hotel when I pass away, I mean. Would you be interested in that?'

Richard didn't know what to say.

'Thank you,' he said eventually. 'Please let me think on this.'

Richard asked Trudy if she had any other nieces and nephews in the family, who might like to take up her offer.

'None here In Africa,' she told him. 'I do have a nephew back in Ireland who I invited out here with a view of taking over the hotel. I'm afraid he was too fond of himself and the ladies around here, especially my staff. After two years, just when I was beginning to trust him and was about to sign things over to him, I caught him in bed with my private nurse. So I shipped him back home to his wife and family. I'm sure he never told them why he came back. My private nurse I let go also. So now my faithful workers take care of me.

'I have been here in Africa for almost forty years,' she continued. 'When I arrived here off the ship, Africa was not like it is now. There were not many women here. It was all men really. It was difficult to integrate with them. They looked down on me being a woman. I had a difficult time convincing them that I could do as well as them, if not better. There was also a problem with suitors looking for my hand in marriage.'

'You never did? Never married?'

Trudy shook her head.

'They thought they only needed to ask, but I was not about to marry anyone. All my energies went into building the hotel. Maybe I just never met the right person.'

'Do you ever regret it?'

'No, I don't regret it. My life could have been very different, I know, but I have been happy, Richard. All these people who depend on me here, they need me. They feel like my family. There are always children here, and I sometimes get the chance to help them with reading and writing and things. I don't feel like I've missed out, not really.'

'You're a remarkable woman.'

'I started out with a site, and waited over two years to get building started. I had to lobby the local politicians and keep my mind sharp because the men here did not want a woman doing a man's job. Or so they thought,' she chuckled. Richard grinned back.

Epilogue

Richard Fitzgerald was so taken with his great-aunt Trudy that he stayed in her hotel while he made investments in the gold mines. Richard was fascinated with her, her courage and commitment to her hotel and her staff. He felt so at home in her company, especially in the evenings, when she would talk to him about her time growing up in rural Ireland. Trudy would also look forward to Richard returning back from his day's work. She told him what she remembered about Bruff, and Richard began to long to go there, although Trudy said it was all probably changed now, especially with the railway from Limerick to Dublin.

The old homestead in Bruff was gone now, and new landlords had taken over the farm and rented it out. The last she heard was that there was a family called O'Keefe living there.

'I never intend to go back to Ireland,' Trudy told Richard.

Richard wrote to his father a long and detailed letter, informing him of his astonishing meeting with Trudy. In his letter, Richard explained how she came to be, how her father had married after his sons left for America. He also relayed how Trudy's mother had died after a fire. He wrote at length of his investments and how the exploration was going. His father's reply took weeks to arrive.

Richard's father was excited to hear about his new and distinguished relative. He told Richard how he would love to travel to Ireland and see the old home place and townland of Bruff, and about how he too had thought through the years about going back to where his father and uncle had grown up.

Richard's father also wanted to meet Trudy, but felt that he was too old for such a voyage. He felt that he did not have the strength, and would probably not make it back to America.

So Richard's father also wrote to Trudy and let her know how happy he was that Richard had met her.

'What were the chances of meeting her in all the world?' he wrote in his letter. 'It's like it was meant to be.'

He congratulated her on her fine hotel, and how she was such a successful businesswoman.

To Richard's delight, his father asked him to travel to Ireland and visit all the places he would visit if he were fit and able to go himself. Richard's father listed out Limerick City and Bruff, and also asked Richard to visit his uncle Martin, who had married a Tipperary girl. Richard's father hoped they were still living. If not, hopefully Richard would meet some of their children. Richard would then return to Boston and give his father all the news personally.

Trudy Fitzgerald had mixed feelings about the trip back home. Richard asked her to accompany him. She declined for the same reasons as his father. She spoke at length to Richard about his voyage to Ireland, and the dangers and the long time at sea.

She handed him an old notebook that she had in her writing-desk.

'Take a look at that,' she said. 'Handle it carefully; it's getting old.'

Trudy had sketched her voyage from Queenstown to Liverpool, and then on to Port Natal. Richard could make out the cliffs of Dover, a dangerous spot for any vessel, and several remarkable countries along the way. He sat back in the chair, amazed.

'My dear great aunt,' he said, 'I am… I'm just in awe of you and how you have lived your life. I will never meet the likes of you again, you are such a pioneer.'

Trudy smiled gently.

'I'm sure you will, Richard.'

Richard wound down his investments and exploration at the Kimberley gold mines. His focus was on his trip to Ireland. The journey took over his every thought. The next available ship was over a month away. He started to plan out his voyage; he would sail to Liverpool just like Trudy, and then stop there for four days to get the next ship to Ireland.

He was a great help in the hotel, and was learning the business very quickly. But it was still not sure if he would return and take over the business. Trudy had a feeling that he would not return to Africa, but would return to his father in Boston.

They were talking as usual by the fire one evening, well into Richard's preparations. Trudy then asked him about returning to her and taking over the hotel.

'Great-aunt,' he said tenderly, 'I am not coming back to South Africa. I will eventually return to my father in Boston. I hope you will get someone else more suitable to take over your precious hotel. I know how hard you have worked to make this a success. I feel that I would not do your hotel justice. I want to be free to work and see Ireland, and who knows how long I will stay there?'

Trudy assured him that she would find the right person to take over the hotel when the time came. For now, she would continue working. She made him promise that he would write to her the day he arrived and keep her up to date on his time there. Trudy then advised Richard to bring some warm clothes for the cold weather at sea and in Ireland too. He was used to the heat of South Africa and was very tanned.

The day came for Richard to go. Trudy was in the foyer of the hotel, waiting for him to come down for his farewell. She threw her arms around him, holding him tightly and wishing him well. She hoped that she would see him again sometime. As he waved to her from the entrance of the hotel, she could see the sadness in his eyes. She would long for the day when she would receive a letter with an Irish postmark.

Richard made the journey to Ireland without any seasickness, finding his sea legs on the very first day. He spent most of his time on deck with the captain, and mapped out the voyage with the captain's help.

The ship entered Queenstown on a bright sunny morning in July. Richard was up on deck and, as the Irish headlands came into view, he developed goosebumps and his heart beat more quickly. The nearer the ship came to land, the more his heart jumped.

It took a while for the ship to dock. Richard was the first to disembark. As his feet touched Irish soil for the first time, a strange mixture of delight and sadness came over him. He stopped for a moment or two to take in the people at the dock and the smell of the fishing boats.

His bag strung over his shoulder, Richard headed for the main street in the town. He checked into Flynn's boarding-house for the night and asked the owner, Rory Flynn, about how he would travel to Limerick and Bruff. Rory Flynn knew someone who had a car, and would contact him and see if he would take Richard to his ancestral home.

That night, Richard went out to O'Connell's pub, just down the street from Flynn's, for a few beers and to meet and talk with the locals. The bar was full of men drinking and smoking cigarettes and pipes. When Richard opened the door, every man turned around to see who was entering. They could see that he was a stranger.

The barman shouted, 'A pint of porter, Sir?'

'That's it!' Richard replied.

Behind the bar on the left-hand side, men were constantly going in and out. Richard went behind the bar to enter the room, but was caught by the neck and shoved out the door. He called the barman over.

'What's going on in there? What's the big secret?' he asked him.

'No man goes in there unless he is invited,' said the barman quietly. 'If I were you, I would keep out.'

That just made Richard more curious. He wanted to find more out about the mysterious group.

He took a seat at the bar. The man sitting beside him started up a conversation.

'Who are you? Where do you come from?' he asked Richard.

Richard replied, 'I'm a yank returning to find my origins.'

'Your origins?' the man replied. 'You mean your ancestors, surely?'

Then Richard asked the man, 'Do you know anything of the Fitzgeralds? They were from Bruff.'

'There are many of that name here in this county,' the man replied. He nodded towards the corner. 'Do you see that ould fellow sitting behind the pillar? Ask him, he knows everyone around there.'

Richard went and introduced himself. The man was happy enough in his company, and he bought two more pints of porter.

'Where are you from?'

'With an accent like mine, I thought you would have guessed.'

'Well there are not too many visitors that come here, so I wouldn't know what accent you have, but I would guess you must be from America or somewhere like that?'

'Yes, Sir, I am from Boston, America.'

When they got chatting, Richard asked him about the area, and more specifically the Fitzgeralds from Bruff.

'They are all gone now, I think. There are none of them left there. I think the farm was taken over, and it's in the O'Keefe name now.'

'What was happening in the room behind the bar?'

'Ah, don't worry about that, it's only a secret meeting for the Republican Army.'

This was a shock to Richard.

'Do they hold meetings in a bar like this? Don't they have a headquarters?'

'No—most of these men are on the run.'

Richard had never heard of the movement before, and was intrigued by the air of mystery surrounding the organisation.

'I must be going. It was nice meeting you. I'm Richard, by the way.'

'Bob.'

On the next morning, the hackney man Thomas came to collect Richard and take him to from Queenstown to Bruff. It was a lovely morning, the air was fresh, a clean breeze coming from the sea.

Thomas cranked up the car, jumped in, and off the two of them went. Richard was friendly, and loved to talk, so the time went quickly. Thomas gave him a running commentary and history on all the landmarks on the way.

Richard was in awe of the landscape. He could see the Galtee mountains in the distance, and kept remarking to Thomas, his driver, on how beautiful everything was. The road itself was narrow, with many potholes, and weeds that grew as big as humans adorned the ditches, which made the road even smaller. Cattle and horses roamed the road, and some goats were tied together and left at the side of the road to eat the hawthorn bushes in the ditches. Thomas kept trying to avoid both animals and weeds. The smell of burning sticks and timber came from the small cottages close to the road, and Richard saw that many of those small homes were missing windows and had holes in the roof.

Richard also noticed the people they passed on the road, and some looked destitute. Many looked forlorn and skinny; some had bad teeth, their eyes exhausted. Women carried babies wrapped up in the colourful shawls they wore over their shoulders, and several of them looked like they had another baby on the way. In addition, many women had a string of older children behind them, who also looked thin, hungry, their hair matted to their heads. With a shock, Richard realised they were probably crawling with fleas and other vermin. Would they ever make it in life, he wondered. What kind of life will they have? Will those children live to grow up and become women and men?

'Oh my God,' he eventually said to Thomas, 'how will those people survive? They look half dead now. Can anyone help them? Feed them, at least?'

'Well, no,' replied Thomas. 'It is unfortunate they are in the position they are in. They have too many children and nothing to feed them.'

Richard also saw some huge mansions, big houses that could not have been more different from the poor cottages. The big houses had coal and turf smells coming from them. Once more he turned to Thomas.

'It's all or nothing,' said Richard. 'Those huge mansions, with fine horses in the fields—those people must know nothing about their neighbours' hardships. Those houses must take a fortune for the upkeep.'

'Oh, the gentry,' said Thomas, 'they don't want for anything. When the poor people go hunting for rabbits in their fields, the owners hunt them out. They wouldn't let them have the wild rabbits and pheasants, even though they don't want them themselves because they wouldn't eat that kind of meat. They want the best cuts of beef and turkey and chicken. Most of them employ cooks, maids and farmhands, pay them almost nothing.'

Richard could feel anger rising up in his chest.

'Jesus,' he said, 'this whole thing has to be put right. Every man, woman and child in this country should not go hungry. It's a devastating situation to be in when you can't take care of your children. Someone in power should come down here and see with their own eyes the poverty these people are going through.'

Richard and Thomas arrived in the County Limerick town of Kilmallock, where they stopped for something to eat, then continued on their way to Bruff. As they approached Bruff, Richard felt a lump fill his throat. Thomas noticed, and asked if he should stop for a moment or two.

'Yes,' replied Richard, and Thomas pulled over to the side of the road to give Richard time to settle himself.

'I don't know what came over me,' he said to Thomas.

'Don't worry at all about that,' Thomas said.

'Sure that could happen to a judge.' Richard laughed at his attempt at an Irish turn of phrase.

Thomas had a good idea where the Fitzgeralds once lived. To be sure, he stopped and asked a young man they passed.

'Yes, Sir,' said the young man, looking at Richard with curiosity. 'That's where the Fitzgeralds used to live. My father knew the family.'

Thomas pulled up the car at the road gate to the house, turned to Richard and said, 'This is where your ancestors came from.'

Richard opened the gate, and walked up the lane, thinking back over all of the details about the lane and the house that Trudy gave him, and stopping to look for anything that she had mentioned.

Richard rounded the bend in the lane, and stood amazed at the fine building in front of him. Nothing seemed to have changed in all the years that had gone by. This was where they came from. He was home.

The End